You thought *regular-size* Democrats
were destroying the country?

ATTACK
OF THE 50 FT.
DEMOCRATS
A NOVEL

R. K. DELKA

Copyright © 2013 R. K. Delka
All rights reserved.
ISBN 978-0-9890091-0-2
First Edition: March 2013

Printed in the U.S.A.
Belliam Books

To my parents, who taught
honesty, generosity, and hard work—
and didn't raise a Democrat.

CHAPTER 1

Captain Bart Brightman struggled to free his hands from the rope that bound them behind the chair. When the morning sun peeked through the tattered shade on the far side of the small hut, he knew he had been at it all night.

His rebel captor paced, muttering to himself in Spanish. He slapped the back of his neck and inspected the squashed bug in his palm. Sweat flowed down his forehead. He undid the top button of his camouflage uniform shirt, removed his holster, and slammed it on the table.

"When are they coming?" he said in a thick Hispanic accent. He unsheathed his dagger and touched the tip of the blade to the prisoner's nose. "I will not ask again."

Brightman ignored the question as he had for the last few hours. The longer he could delay, the better chance he had of getting his hands free--it was clear his captor wasn't willing, or didn't have permission, to get more forceful.

As he continued working the rope, he looked deliberately at the rebel's shirt and the letters D.U.M.I. stitched on the pocket. He grinned. "Sorry, dummy, I don't know."

The rebel looked at the letters, struggling to read them upside down. "I ... Iwu ... Imud?" He kicked a metal trashcan across the room and forced a slew of Spanish curses through clenched teeth.

But he quickly composed himself when he noticed that a man dressed in a double-breasted tan pinstriped suit, polished wingtip shoes, and a maroon velvet fedora was standing in the doorway. A leather satchel hung from his shoulder. Behind him was a slight man with an unassuming look.

The rebel returned his knife to its sheath and rushed to the well-dressed man. "Señor Joros," he said. "My apologies. I did not know you were there."

Scourge Joros was a titan of the American fashion industry who chose to use his money and influence in the world of politics. Little was known about him and he liked it that way. In fact, he demanded it. When a news story had the nerve to publish his birthday--October, 31--the billionaire with a penchant for social justice executed a hostile takeover and immediately shut the paper down. It was the first, and last, time his name ever appeared in the media.

"Did he talk?" Joros asked.

"No," the rebel said. "He is tough. Very tough. I don't think we will get anything out of him. It seems he would rather die than talk."

Joros pulled a three-legged stool in front of Brightman and sat. "It is not 'dummy,' he sneered. "It is simply the letters D-U-M-I."

"That would be 'dummy.'"

"No," Joros said. "If anything it would be 'doomy.' Perhaps 'doomeye.' But it is not a word. They are just initials. D-U-M-I: Democrats Under My Influence."

"They aren't Democrats, they're socialist rebels."

"Tomato, tomahto. Socialist rebels, Democrats."

"It still spells 'dummy.'"

Joros sighed in annoyance. "I suppose you could read it that way, but I didn't notice until after the shirts were made. Enough of this."

He removed a video camera from his bag, then placed it on the table, pointed it at Brightman, and pressed the "Record" button. "We will get the information out of you sooner or later," Joros said. "It is in your best interest if you make it sooner."

Brightman remained silent. His men were out there, and nothing would make him jeopardize their safety. He wouldn't turn on them, and he wouldn't turn on his country. The rebel was right. He would rather die than talk.

Joros took a pair of latex gloves from his jacket pocket and pulled them onto his hands. "Give me the truth serum," he said to the man that accompanied him.

The man placed a syringe in Joros's palm. Joros held it up, squeezing the bottom until a single drop of fluid overflowed from the tip. "Now," he said to Brightman, "you will talk."

"What's the point?" Brightman asked. He knew it was a stupid question, but it was the first thing that popped into his mind and he needed to buy more time. The rope around his left hand was loosening.

Joros relaxed. He seemed to enjoy the question. "Once you give me the information, my rebels will drive back your forces and take over this government. Then, I will control the country."

"For what purpose?" Another dumb question, but his thumb was almost free.

"The purpose is practice."

"Practice?"

"Yes," Joros said, rolling up Brightman's sleeve to reveal his right bicep. He lifted the needle to the captain's arm, then paused and lowered it.

"I think it is high time there are more victors for the world's spoils. That, of course, cannot happen with the political, social, and economic structures we currently suffer. It can only be achieved through fundamental transformation. Unfortunately, fundamentally transforming the world is not easy. But, after some practice on a couple of smaller countries, one could transform a larger country. The USA, for instance."

Brightman's blood boiled. To a man who had dreamed of serving his country since childhood, following in his father's and grandfather's footsteps, Joros's words were enraging. "We have laws," he said. "A governing document. It's not the kind of country you can just walk into and take control of."

Joros smirked. "You're governed by people, and people are far more weak-minded than you give them credit for."

Brightman shook his head at his captor's arrogance. "I suppose you have some kind of control over the weak-minded?"

"I have a gift," Joros said, lifting his chin in the air. He brought the needle back up to Brightman's arm. "This will hurt a bit less than I would like it to."

Brightman gave one last, strong twist.

His left hand came free. He swung it around hard, landing it on Joros's head and knocking him to the ground. Then he lunged at the rebel, sending him reeling back. He grabbed the gun from the table, shoved it into his beltline, and then kicked the door open.

A wave of thick, humid air pounded him as he rushed outside and raced across the dirt road, toward the jungle.

A commotion arose as rebels followed, but Brightman continued into the thick brush, slapping heavy leaves and thick branches out of the way as he forged his own trail. Every step drained strength from his already weakened body.

He stopped at a clearing where a dirt road ran left to right in front of him. He would be a clear target in the openness as he tried to cross. But if he made it, and the rebels followed, they would be in the open, giving him a clear shot.

He sprinted across as bullets flew by.

When he reached the other side, he dove, head first, over a fallen tree. He scrambled to his knees and peered over the log, steadying his weapon on top of it, waiting for his enemies to cross.

But they didn't. They stopped and scattered, taking cover in the brush.

For now, the temporary standoff was the best Brightman could hope for, and he took the opportunity to rest. If he started to run again, the rebels would follow--and it was a race he was sure to lose.

He kept his eyes glued to the jungle across the road, monitoring the movements of his enemies by the way the leaves rustled. As the minutes passed, there were more rustles--reinforcements were coming.

***

*** SPECIAL EVENT ***

*** FRANK FRANKLIN REPORTING ***

*** BEGIN OFFICIAL TRANSCRIPT ***

FRANK FRANKLIN: Good evening, America, I'm Frank Franklin, inside The Broadway Theatre.

I'm here with Suzie Jane, winner of the Tony Award for best actress. Suzie, your portrayal of a typical white woman in the hit musical *Coming Home to Roost* was groundbreaking. How did you prepare for the role?

SUZIE JANE: Well, I actually am a white woman. But not a typical one, so it wasn't easy. I had to push aside everything I had learned over the course of my life and, basically, unlearn it all.

FRANK FRANKLIN: A lot of hard work, I'm sure. I imagine this award is something you have been dreaming of your whole life.

SUZIE JANE: Actually, when I was a little girl I dreamed of winning a Nobel Prize.

FRANK FRANKLIN: Well, you should be proud. They don't give a Tony just anyone, you know.

SUZIE JANE: I know. I am proud and I'd like to thank--

FRANK FRANKLIN: Let me switch topics here for a moment. Earlier in the week, at this very theater, you dedicated one of your performances to a very special, courageous group of people. Let's talk about that.

SUZIE JANE: There is a group of fighters, freedom fighters--let's be accurate--down in the central and south Americas. They are valiantly fighting their oppressors.

FRANK FRANKLIN: And their oppressors are?

SUZIE JANE: (LAUGHS) I think you're goading me.

FRANK FRANKLIN: (LAUGHS) Just a little.

SUZIE JANE: We are the oppressors. Okay, now you got me started so I'm going to rant. But I hate to talk bad about our country.

FRANK FRANKLIN: No, that's okay.

SUZIE JANE: Well, we are imposing our capitalism on them because the ruling class in this country thinks that it will solve the world's problems. But it won't. What our worship of materialism boils down to is dirtier air and dirtier water--an environment where nothing can survive.

A perfect example--we know now that the albino gorilla, indigenous to that area, is extinct. It was the most beautiful animal you have ever seen. A few years ago there were still a couple, but now they are all dead.

FRANK FRANKLIN: And our soldiers' conduct in this conflict has been disgraceful.

SUZIE JANE: Um, is that a question?

FRANK FRANKLIN: Oh. I mean, what do you make of our soldiers' conduct?

SUZIE JANE: Well, we've all heard the stories of them destroying villages and that sort of thing. If it's true--

FRANK FRANKLIN: It is. I mean, what if it is?

SUZIE JANE: If that sort of thing is true then I don't see how we can support our government in this.

FRANK FRANKLIN: It's hard to be proud of this country.

SUZIE JANE: Question?

FRANK FRANKLIN: I mean, is it hard to be proud of the country?

SUZIE JANE: It is hard right now. But I hope that, at some point in my adult life, I can be proud of it again.

FRANK FRANKLIN: I can't see that happening. I mean, can I see that happening? Wait. Never mind. You know, sometimes--excuse me-- what is that man doing over there? Why is he sorting through that trash can?

Security!

SUZIE JANE: Him again? Hey, is that--that's my old lipstick he took from there.

(SECURITY GUARDS CHASE MAN)

FRANK FRANKLIN: Okay, security is on his tail now.

SUZIE JANE: I'm sorry. You know, that kind of freaks me out. I'd like to end this interview.

8

FRANK FRANKLIN: Okay. Well, Suzie Jane,
everyone. The Tony Award-winning typical
white woman.

*** END TRANSCRIPT ***

***

Dr. Albert Gress raced out of the theater and onto Broadway. He navigated through the crowded street and sprinted down 7th Avenue to the subway entrance. When he finally stopped to catch his breath, he turned and peered down the road.

The security guards were nowhere in sight.

He headed down the steps and took the E line to Penn Station where he settled into a seat on the express train to Washington, D.C.

From his jacket pocket, he pulled out Suzie Jane's lipstick. A single twist of the bottom pushed up a small chunk of ruby red. He smiled.

Suzie Jane was one of the finest female specimens of her time. With electric-blue eyes, full pouty lips, and tight-curled auburn hair, her DNA was remarkable--and there was sure to be enough of it on the lipstick for Gress to work with. He had extracted genetic sequences from far smaller samples.

He twisted the small tube closed and returned it to his pocket, then relaxed his head against the seat and fell into deep thought--to a future when his work had changed the world and genetic imperfections no longer plagued mankind.

***

Rebels continued to pour into the jungle on the other side of the road.

"He's behind the log," one called out in Spanish.

"Over there," said another.

The undergrowth rattled as enemy soldiers scurried, staking out their positions and poking their gun barrels through the leaves. When the influx stopped and the rebels settled, silence and stillness set in.

Brightman assessed the landscape, trying to formulate an escape, but he quickly realized there was none. Exhausted, he had no chance of outrunning his enemies.

As that fact sunk in, a soft voice came from the right side, down the dirt path. A young local boy, about eight, sang as he strolled along. He rested a fishing rod on his shoulder with one hand and carried a bucket in the other. As the barefoot boy passed, he stepped on something that caused him to jump and shriek. Crying, he sat down in the middle of the road and inspected his foot.

"Son," called a man in Spanish from further down the left side of the road. "Hurry. Come now."

The child, focused on his foot, ignored his father's calls.

An engine roared from beyond the boy. A jeep approached. A cloud of dirt arose as the speeding vehicle came nearer.

Brightman knew the child wouldn't move in time. He knew the jeep wouldn't stop in time. Instinct pushed him out from behind the log. He raced toward the boy, scooped him up, and ran toward the father.

A flurry of bullets filled the air as the rebels resumed the chase.

Brightman handed the boy off to the father without breaking stride and continued down the road. But in the split second that he had passed the man, the two locked eyes. The gratefulness of the stranger shined through and Brightman, sure his time was coming to an end, basked in the pride of his final deed.

His legs were getting weaker with every step, but he willed them to keep moving, trying to outpace his shadow that floated on the ground in front of him.

The bullets continued, accompanied by footsteps and yelling as the rebels chased.

"West, West," came a call from behind. "Go West, young man."

Brightman remembered the look in the stranger's eyes and knew it was him. A small path came into view on the left--the west. He reached out for the trunk of a thin tree and catapulted himself into the turn.

Ahead, there was a river. A small motorboat floated at its bank.

He raced to the boat and jumped in, then turned and fired a shot into the small crowd that followed.

The rebels scattered.

Brightman yanked the pull cord and the engine screamed as the boat jumped forward, kicking up water as it left the shore. He turned to fire his remaining bullets as the boat glided over the river, quickly putting distance between him and the land. He coasted for a while, turning to look back every few minutes.

The river was quiet.

As the sun lifted higher into the sky, it beat down hard, evaporating what little energy he had left. He fixed himself into a comfortable position on the boat's floor, then lowered his head, unable to keep his eyes open.

***

Click.

The barrel of an assault rifle dug into Brightman's cheek, waking him and pinning his head against the floor of the marooned boat.

"Get up," the gunman said in his familiar accent. Two other men, also armed and aiming, stood behind. They marched Brightman to a pickup truck a hundred feet inland and threw him into the open bed. The Hispanic father, guarded by two more armed rebels, was already there.

As the truck bounced and bounded down the dirt road, Brightman studied the man who had tried to save him.

He was thin, with weathered dark skin and messy black hair. His shirt, unbuttoned down to the fourth button, allowed a half-circle shaped medallion--a U.S. silver dollar crudely cut down the middle--to hang freely from his neck on a hemp string. He appeared to be a poor villager and would surely be killed for helping an American. But Brightman could see in the man's eyes that there was no regret, that he was simply repaying, with loyalty and honor, for saving his son.

Brightman leaned into the man, keeping his eyes on the guards, and spoke loud, above the roar of the engine. "Where is the boy?" he said in Spanish.

"He ran," the man said in English. "He runs fast."

The man smiled.

Brightman smiled too. "You speak English?"

The villager pulled a small softcover book from his back pocket. "I learn. With this."

The book's cover was worn and torn. The spine was cracked. The title, <u>Famous American Quotations</u>, was barely discernible due to the faded writing and embedded dirt.

"Someday," the man said, "I will go to America. My family will be free."

A guard jabbed the barrel of his semi-automatic between the two men. "Separate." He ripped the book from the villager's hand and tossed it over the side. The pages flapped and fluttered as it sailed into the jungle that lined the road.

As the rebels looked to each other and laughed, the Hispanic man buttoned his shirt higher, hiding the cut silver dollar necklace.

They drove the remainder of the thirty-minute trip in silence. When the truck stopped, the rebels manhandled Brightman out of the back.

He turned, struggling to see the fate of his companion, but the rebels pushed the captain forward, bringing him to the same room he had escaped from earlier. They tied him to the chair with his hands behind his back, weaving the rope in one long piece around his neck, chest, and wrists.

Jorcs entered, nursing a bruise above his right eye with a red silk handkerchief. He grabbed the rope and gave a hard yank.

It choked the prisoner, pushing the air out of his lungs as it sank into the skin on his wrists. He struggled for a brief moment but quickly realized it was futile. He sat, stiff and tense, looking straight ahead.

Joros started the video camera, then took the syringe from the table and pulled the stool next to Brightman. He rolled up the soldier's sleeve and slid the needle into his upper arm, injecting the truth serum.

A strange, light feeling came over the prisoner. He relaxed, and found his mind wandering even as he tried to focus on his captors. He thought back to when he was a young child playing army with the neighborhood kids. He thought of the Hispanic father who had tried to save him by giving up his boat. He thought of all of the times between those two events. The memories flowed through him with ease, without inhibitions.

"Now," Joros said. "When will they arrive?"

CHAPTER 2

TWENTY-FIVE YEARS LATER

Senator Brightman pounded his fist on the oak door. "Open up," he said, his coarse voice fighting its way through gritted teeth.

His colleague, Senate Minority Leader Barney Jaxon, opened the door. "Hey," he said in a soft tone, his shoulders slumped.

Brightman glared at the young Republican and barreled his way to the center of the room. "I hear everyone has done an about face and plans to vote in favor of this bill tomorrow. This 'Military Cooperation Act' or whatever they're calling it. Is that true?"

Jaxon set his eyes on the floor and shrugged.

"This bill will neuter our military," Brightman said. "Hell, it'll eliminate it."

"There hasn't been a war in twenty years," Jaxon said, still looking at the ground. "Not even a threat. Not even the threat of a threat. No police action. No contingency operation. Nothing." He finally lifted his head and met Brightman's eyes. "The old way of doing things just doesn't work anymore."

"So weakness works? This progressive nightmare we're living in works? Is that what you're telling me?"

"Well ... kinda."

Brightman sighed. This wasn't the first time he had this kind of conversation with a member of his party. It was, however, the first time he had asked the question in such blunt terms. The equally blunt answer only partially surprised him.

"Look," Jaxon said. "It's not like we're going to vote for every Democrat-led bill that comes along. I mean, we need a two-party system. Otherwise, we're all out of a job. I get that. But on this one it's just not worth it."

"The public doesn't want this. Are you ready to explain your vote to your constituents?"

"I won't have to. It's going to be, you know, low profile."

Brightman looked at him with suspicion. "What do you mean 'low profile'?"

"The vote's going to be moved. We're doing it next week. A special session, I think."

"When next week?"

Jaxon looked at the ground again. "The fourth. I think," he mumbled. "A memo is going out later."

Brightman shook his head in disbelief. "You're going to vote on a military-busting bill on the Fourth of July? And the others agree?"

"They agree that they don't want to end up like you."

"Like me?" Suddenly it all made sense. The bullying media had them shaking in their boots. He stepped toward Jaxon. "You mean the most hated man in Washington?"

Jaxon took a small step back and remained silent.

"Or is it the most hated man in America?" Brightman

pointed his finger at his colleague. "Don't make the mistake of thinking you can trust these guys. They're vultures. When it suits them to use you as their target they won't care one bit how you voted on this bill or any other one for that matter."

He figured this line of reasoning, coming from him, resonated. If anyone knew the brutal, dragged-through-the-mud treatment the media was capable of inflicting, he did. Everyone in Washington knew full well what he had been through.

"It doesn't matter what the reason is," Jaxon said. "We wouldn't have the votes to stop it anyway. We haven't had the votes for anything in four years."

Brightman seethed. But it was true. They *hadn't* had the votes for anything in four years. And during those years, not a day passed where he didn't blame himself for the state of his party and, by extension, his country.

He paused to let his anger simmer. "What will it take to get you to do the right thing on this, and not the easy thing?"

Jaxon shrugged. "It's easy for you. You don't have to worry about re-election." He continued with an innocent confusion, "You're retiring. Why does it even matter to you?"

Why does it matter? Brightman had asked himself that question from time to time over the last few years, usually after he came out on the losing end of a vote which, recently, happened often. It wasn't the electorate. That much he was sure of as they clearly no use for him.

The answer was simple. He couldn't make it not matter. If he could, he would. Over the last four years he had watched as the country slid further from the ideals it was founded on and closer to the point of not being able to return to them. But he still held out hope.

"The rest of us have a good thing going on here," Jaxon said. "We're not going to throw it all away on one dumb vote."

Brightman cringed as the words hit his ears. He summoned every bit of self-control to keep from exploding. With a deep, slow breath he left the room, closing the door gently behind him.

**

The Capitol's hallway buzzed. Camera crews jockeyed for position as reporters grabbed the nearest politician for a quick interview.

As Brightman stepped through the chaos, he scanned the area. His eyes landed on Merv Nutley, the media weasel who evoked Brightman's resentment more than any other.

The senator willed his eyes to burn a hole through the man but, unfortunately, Nutley didn't burst into flames and drop into a pile of ash right there in the middle of the corridor. Of course, if he had, Brightman would have gladly kicked the pile and scattered the ashes across the floor.

A hard slam on the back thrust Brightman forward. Colonel Stupp, his old friend and combat buddy, caught up and walked alongside him. An unlit Gran Corona extended from his mouth.

"It's over," Brightman said in a morose tone. "Pretty soon our military won't have two nickels to rub together. Before you know it we won't even have a military."

"They're not getting me out of there," Stupp said, the

cigar clenched between his teeth. "I'm not going anywhere until there are stars on these shoulders."

"The funding is going to dry up soon."

"I know. They started preparing a few months ago, tagging jets and other crap to decommission." He leaned into Brightman and spoke softly. "But I kept one for myself."

"You kept one what for yourself?"

Stupp looked around, then spoke in a whisper. "An FT-15 fighter jet."

Brightman stopped in his tracks and dropped his jaw. "What? What do you mean you kept one?"

"Shh," Stupp said, looking around again. "There's an old hangar in the rear compound that hasn't been touched in decades. It's got an FT-15 in perfect working order. I'm the only one who knows about it."

"Give me a break," Brightman said. "These Dems missed taking something from defense?"

"It was lost years ago," Steel said, emphasizing the word lost with sarcasm. "I made sure of that." A wry smile crawled onto his face. "And I'm the only one on the base with clearance."

"I don't want to hear any more," Brightman said.

"She's a beauty," Stupp said. "Just like we flew back in the day."

Brightman held up his hands. "I didn't hear a thing."

"Gotcha. Well, I know you did what you could in there. It seems every battle is a loser now."

"It's gonna get worse," Brightman said, stopping in front of his office door. "Have you seen the polls, the Democrats are leading just about everywhere?"

"Polls?" Stupp gave an incredulous look. With his arms

hanging at his side, he used his lips to pull his cigar forward, bit off a small chunk, and then spit the piece out before maneuvering the stogie back to its original position. "That's your world, pal. My world is FT-15s."

Brightman kicked his foot, flinging off the slimy chunk of tobacco that had landed on it.

"Talk to you later, buddy," Stupp said. He walloped Brightman on the shoulder before heading down the hall.

Brightman turned to watch his friend walk away. He focused on the handless stumps at the end of the colonel's arms. The familiar but uneasy feeling hit his stomach as it always did when he looked at the end of Stupp's stumps. On the surface, he knew it wasn't his fault, but deep down he still felt guilty about it, even twenty-five years later. How could he not? Had he been able to resist the truth serum, Stupp's plane would never have been shot down and his friend would still have his hands.

Further down the hall, Stupp stopped and turned back to Brightman. "If you want a ride, just ring me," he said, a wicked smile still on his face. He held his stumps in the air. "Of course, you'll have to drive."

***

*** BREAKING NEWS ***

*** STEVE STEVENS REPORTING ***

*** BEGIN OFFICIAL TRANSCRIPT ***

STEVE STEVENS: Good morning, America, I'm Steve Stevens. I hope everyone is recovering well from a festive Independence Day.

Of course, not everyone was able to enjoy the holiday. Our hardworking public officials put in some overtime last night and, as the clock struck midnight, the Senate passed the North American Military Cooperation Act on a ninety-nine to one vote.

A short time later, President Puppit signed the bill into law. (DEEP SIGH) Does that man even know the meaning of the word "rest"?

Excuse me for a moment, this itching is-- it's been just driving me crazy lately. Our regular viewers out there are aware of my, uh, mysterious itching. No diagnosis for it yet. But I do want to thank everyone for your suggestions on dealing with this. Your emails and letters have been tremendously supportive. Okay, it seems to be all scratched now.

We haven't spoken much about NAMCA in the months leading up to this vote. But now that the bill has been passed, there's no better time to find out what's in it. It's one of the major accomplishments of President Puppit's first term and--excuse me, sometimes this itching comes right back.

If you can hold on a second, I just want to grab this. Let me hold this up to the camera. Can you zoom in on that? Perfect.

This is a back scratcher one of our viewers sent in recently. It's nice. Hand carved. I think that's oak. If you look at it, there's a picture of Senator Brightman's face sort of etched in there. Can you see that? And the engraving along here, I love this, it says "use this to scratch your butt." Thought that was kind of funny. Anyway, let me just scratch away for a minute.

Okay, I think we're all good now.

It's important that we understand NAMCA's benefits when we head to the polls in a couple of weeks, so let's dive right in. Now, I have the bill here, and I'll just jump to a random page. Okay, I'm on page 4,827. Let's see what we have.

(READING FROM TEXT OF THE BILL): Proper redemption of tangible defense assets to be determined by a committee, of direct appointment by the president of the United States, and shall include, but not be limited to, actions of an inducing or subsidiary nature as they pertain to any and all subjects and or obligations described in section 2203, subsection b, paragraph 19.

Whew. Now, what exactly is being said here, um, I really don't know. So, I'd like to welcome our political analyst, Carl Jones, to break it down for us. Carl, what is it saying?

CARL JONES (POLITICAL ANALYST): It's

actually very simple. The paragraph alludes to section 2203, subsection b, paragraph 19, which lays out the details of proposed government spending for alternative energy--wind energy, specifically. The passage you read is saying that tangible defense assets, that would most likely be the big stuff like planes and tanks and such, will be disassembled, and their parts recycled and used for windmills.

STEVE STEVENS: Windmills? Fantastic! Let's stop wasting all our money on guns and things, right? Just this morning it was windy as all heck as I was coming to work. Very windy. And windmills would be good to capture that wind, right?

CARL JONES: Absolutely. And it's also good policy.

STEVE STEVENS: That's true. And the proof, of course, can be seen in the Senate vote. It was almost unanimous.

CARL JONES: Almost. I think we all know who the lone dissenter was but I don't see any reason to dwell on that. I mean, he accounts for only 1 percent of the Senate. It's fair to say he probably represents only 1 percent of the country.

STEVE STEVENS: You mean the 1 percent that wants to throw all of our money into guns and blowing things up?

CARL JONES: Exactly.

STEVE STEVENS (MOCKING TONE): Oh no, the

bad guys are coming. We need guns and big, loud fighting thingies. Let's blow stuff up. Boom, boom, boom.

(LAUGHTER)

STEVE STEVENS: Okay, thanks Carl. Thanks for being with us. So there it is. Another transformational law passed by President Puppit.

Where did I put that scratcher?

*** END TRANSCRIPT ***

***

"Senator. Natanio Halendros. We've got some things I think you would be interested in. Give me a call."

Brightman tapped the delete button on his phone, erasing the voicemail. Natanio Halendros had been calling every couple of months for the past three years. The messages he left ranged from requesting Brightman to appear at conservative grassroots events to offers for collaborating on startup organizations.

He wasn't quite sure why he had never returned any of the phone calls. There was no doubt that Halendros and his group of patriots, Constitution Verbatim, were his kind of small-government conservatives. Maybe it was a fear of getting his hopes up that there were still people who loved the country as much as he did, only to be let down. But the reason didn't matter. This was his final term. In a couple of months he would be retired, and the country's problems would no longer be his problems.

The shelves on the wall were cluttered with memorabilia from a lifetime of public service. Like the rest of the things in the office, it should already have been packed in the cardboard boxes that lay unopened in the corner, but he hadn't had a chance.

He picked up a silver dollar medallion that had been crudely cut in half and ran his finger along the rough-cut edge. As he remembered the Hispanic man who gave it to him so many years ago, he hung the medallion on his neck from its hemp string.

Reaching to the back of the top shelf, he grabbed the round, blue and red pin that rested behind a picture frame. He wiped off a thin layer of dust and gazed at the words "Brightman For President" written in bold white letters. Then, as he had done a million times, he went over his fall from grace in his mind.

As a bonafide war hero, he had cruised into the Senate, and then re-election, with landslide victories. Four years ago, his ascendancy to the highest office in the land was all but a sure thing. His campaign was firing on all cylinders. Fundraising was through the roof. Poll numbers were solid.

Then the video.

The video taken in South America twenty-five years ago that showed him spilling his guts and betraying his country.

His political enemies, and their accomplices in the media, played it perfectly. Brightman went from hero to hated almost instantly, bringing a myriad of Republicans across the country down with him.

He sat and spun in his chair to look out his office window. Whether in the military or in politics, he had spent his entire life in public service. But the fire was gone. Soon enough, he would be back home, relaxing, spending his days in serene privacy.

He clutched the pin tight, spun back toward his desk, and looked over at the cardboard boxes in the corner. He thought about starting to pack, then tossed the pin on the desk and turned back toward the window.

CHAPTER 3

Merv Nutley sat on the examination room table and tried to remember the last time his left leg didn't tingle. He couldn't. He tried to pinpoint the exact day it had started but, as his thoughts cascaded back in time, the days with a tingle turned to weeks, then months, and finally years. About four years. The best he could figure, he had lived with this tingle, day in and day out, for the last four years.

Occasionally, it heated up and caused a burning sensation with considerable pain. A few times, the burning increased and the leg went completely numb, sending him tumbling to the ground if he dared walk on it. But most of the time it was simply a slight, bearable tingle.

The examination room door swung open. "I have to be completely honest," Doctor Schwartz said, entering the room and pulling the manila file from the rack on the outside of the door. "There is no medical explanation for the tingling in your leg."

Nutley dropped his head, not really surprised at the news. Dr. Schwartz was the twelfth and final doctor on his list. From one doctor to the next, Nutley held out hope. "Maybe the next guy will know," he thought each time. But this was the end of the line. If Schwartz didn't know, there was no place else to turn.

A sense of desperation, tinged with fear, built up inside

him. The crinkly white paper beneath him crumpled as he fidgeted. "But it must be something," he said, his voice shaking. "Something must be causing this."

"Of course it's something," the doctor said. He paused, carefully collecting the words for his next sentence.

"What?" Nutley said, growing nervous as the doctor hesitated. "What are you thinking?" The bad news was coming. He could feel it. "Cancer? Lou Gehrig's? Lupus? Just tell me!"

"There simply doesn't seem to be anything wrong with you--"

"Okay, you said that already. Every doctor I've been to has said that."

"Physically," the doctor continued.

"Physically, what?"

"There doesn't seem to be anything wrong with you, *physically*."

Nutley let the words sink in. A slight chuckle slipped out. "You're telling me there's something wrong with me mentally?"

"Mentally is not the right word. I would prefer ... subconsciously."

"What do you mean subconsciously?"

"How do I put this?" Dr. Schwartz said. "I suspect that you simply have a good old-fashioned man crush."

Nutley let another chuckle slip out. Then another, followed by a full laugh. "That's ridiculous."

"Is it?"

"Yes, it is. I mean, now you're a shrink?"

"Actually, I spent a number of years practicing

psychiatry before I switched to neurology. I've seen my fair share of this. There are many physical manifestations, and the tingling in your leg is not an uncommon one."

"I'm not gay." Nutley shook his head, dismissing the idea. He couldn't believe what this man was implying. He looked at the framed degrees and certifications hanging on the wall. Clearly, the doctor was no dummy, but he was certainly sounding like one.

"I've been married," he said. "Five times."

Dr. Schwartz opened Nutley's medical chart and began to write in it.

"To a woman," Nutley continued. "Every time." He leaned forward, peering over the doctor's arm, trying to see what he was writing.

The doctor flipped the chart closed and tossed it on the table. "I'm going to refer you to Dr. Matthews. He is an excellent psychiatrist--and a true expert in the matter of man-crushes. I have no doubt he'll be able to help you."

"Don't waste your time. I'm not gay."

"This does not mean you're gay. But you must identify the object of your desire and find a way to deal with your man love."

"And if I can't?"

"Then it may get worse."

"Worse? Last week I was doing an interview with the president of the United States and my leg went completely numb. Numb. Completely. The president of the United States." He rubbed his leg as a tingle heated up. "Do you have any idea how embarrassing it was when I stood to leave and then fell into the safety of the president's strong arms?"

The burning sensation grew hotter. He clutched his thigh.

"It was humiliating. How could it get worse?" He released his leg, now completely numb. "Wait a second. Why am I even entertaining this? I do not have a man crush."

He pushed himself off the table, took a step, and fell to the floor.

***

Sitting in the swivel chair on the set of his daily news show, Merv Nutley took three slow breaths to relax his body. It did nothing, however, to soothe his racing mind.

Pat Maddle was riding his heels. Lately, it seemed every corner of the office and every pundit in town was mentioning the rookie's name for one reason or another. He knew Maddle didn't have half his journalistic instinct or talent. But what he knew didn't matter. What mattered was what everyone else thought. And everyone else thought Maddle was a rising star, good enough, maybe, to take his place. If he was going to leave the rookie in the dust, he could only do it with great journalism. Tonight, that meant nailing his right-wing extremist guest, Natanio Halendros, to the cross.

"On the air in three, two, one." The cameraman's bony index finger pointed to Nutley as the "On Air" sign lit up. The stagehands, directors, and other members of the production team scurried around offstage.

Nutley looked into camera number one. "Thanks for joining me on tonight's edition of Tough Nut where we ask the tough questions and tackle the big problems. We have a lot to cover tonight. Later, we'll be airing part one of my interview with President Obie Puppit."

The moment the words "President Obie Puppit" left his lips, the scene of himself falling into the president's arms played in his mind's eye. The tingle in his leg heated up, and the pins and needles pulled him back to reality.

"We will also get into the benefits of the North American Military Cooperation Act, or NAMCA. It recently passed the Senate with a ninety-nine to one vote. We'll explore the many ways it's going to make the country safer, while spending a fraction of what we used to spend on defense."

He switched his gaze to camera number two. "But first, our guest, Natanio Halendros, a man who agrees with the one percent of senators who voted against NAMCA. He is also the founder of the right-wing extremist group, Constitution Verbatim, a group that is apparently against us being safer. Mr. Halendros, welcome."

"We are not against us being safer," Halendros said with a slight hint of an Hispanic accent. "But we do value the traditions of our country's founders."

"President Puppit argues that NAMCA make us stronger," Nutley said. And with those words, the tingle in his leg gained strength. For a brief second, the scene of himself falling into the president's arms returned to his head. What was I saying? "Um, the North American Military Cooperation Act. Yes. We would be entering into an agreement with two other North American countries, pooling our resources. That means our money, our equipment, and our intelligence would be three times as strong, for only one-third the cost. Are you also against math?"

Halendros shook his head and gave a slight chuckle. "Look, the notion that Mexico and Canada are going to put into this agreement the same as we are is ridiculous. The United States has the most exceptional military on the planet. Our neighbors, with all due respect, do not."

"I think our neighbors would argue that their military is just as exceptional to them as ours is to us."

"They might, but it simply isn't true. Ronald Reagan once said--"

"Here we go again," Nutley said, throwing his arms into the air. "What is the fascination you people have with that man?"

"To quote President Reagan," Halendros continued, "there are some who've forgotten why we have a military. It's not to promote war. It's to be prepared for peace."

Nutley rolled his eyes. "How quaint."

"I think our representatives have forgotten why we have a military."

"Let's look at history," Nutley said. "If you go back to our founding, we cooperated with other countries tremendously. We wouldn't have won the Revolution without the help of France. We wouldn't have won World War II without the Allies. Yet, it seems Constitution Verbatim advocates a go-it-alone strategy. We're living in a global world now. This isn't the 1700s or the eighteenth century."

"And the world is an even more dangerous place than it was back then, precisely because of how global it is."

"There hasn't been a war in years," Nutley said. "And thanks to President Puppit we can be sure that--" a hot bolt shot through his leg. He kicked, as if a small animal was clutching his foot.

"Mr. Nutley, I come from a country that, among

other things, used its military ..."

As Nutley continued kicking his leg, an image of President Puppit graced a large monitor. Once again, the embarrassing moment of falling into the president's arms played out in his mind. The tingling intensified and grew hotter. He pressed his hand to his leg. It was numb. Completely numb. A man crush. How ridiculous.

As Halendros continued speaking, Nutley studied him. Maybe he was Mexican. Or Cuban. Whatever. Halendros was a handsome enough man--thick dark hair, olive skin, nice smile. But Nutley wasn't attracted to him. Not at all. A man crush. Nonsense.

He looked at the stagehands at the other end of the room. Most of them were men, and some of them were good looking. He could admit that. He squinted and focused on them, his eyes jumping from one to the next, daring himself to feel something. Nothing. Of course not.

Suddenly, his entire body went numb. Not from a tingling but from a paralyzing fear. He was on national television and had just spent the last who-knows-how-long in a daydream. What in the world had he been talking about with Halendros? He focused his attention back on his guest.

"... You have to agree with that," Halendros said.

Nutley stared, unblinking, into camera number one. His mind was empty, but he had to say something. "Um, well, yeah, sure."

The jostling and scurrying on the other side of the set stopped cold. The entire room turned their attention to the host. The stagehands, interns, and all of the other workers stood frozen with wide eyes and dropped jaws.

"You do?" Halendros said. "I guess we can agree on

something after all." He smiled. "You know, all I want for my kids is to make sure the American Dream ..."

Nutley felt all eyes on him. He scanned the room. From one end to the other, every person in sight looked back at him, bewildered. He turned again to Halendros.

"... I don't see why we can't agree on that as well," Halendros said.

"Mm-hmm," Nutley said. "I guess."

Nutley's assistant, Billy Sample, jumped up and down as he ran his finger across his throat, signaling to go to break.

"And now, let's, um, have a word from our sponsors," Nutley said.

The "On Air" light shut off.

Halendros put his hand on Nutley's shoulder. "Thanks, man. I gained a whole new respect for you today."

Nutley buried his face in his hands and slumped down in his chair. He had just agreed with a right-wing extremist about something. He wasn't sure what that something was, but it didn't matter. Halendros was a political nemesis and agreeing on anything with such a man was career suicide.

***

Scourge Joros sat at the head of the mahogany table in the conference room on the top floor of the MSM News building. Tim Shepherd, the company's founder and chief executive, sat at the right side of the table.

"I expect better from you," Joros said, laying open a

red silk handkerchief with a gold monogram. "MSM is the gold standard. Every media organization in the country follows your lead."

"I'm sorry, sir," Shepherd said, wiping beads of sweat from his forehead. "I assure you this was an isolated incident, and I promise it will not happen again." He turned to steal a quick glance at the two imposing men in black suits stationed on either side of the door.

Joros folded the handkerchief from corner to corner, forming a triangle, then folded two corners to the center. "How have you handled it?"

"Well, we have already spoken with him, sir, and he knows--"

Joros shot his head up from the work in front of him. "You have spoken with him? You do realize how little weight words carry?"

"Well, yes, of course." Shepherd's voice cracked. He forced a weak, awkward laugh. "I mean, you know what they say, actions speak louder--"

"Get rid of him," Joros said as he returned his attention to his silk accessory, folding the last corner toward the top and smoothing out the final product. He placed the handkerchief inside the pocket of his starched white shirt, adjusted the triangle to point upward, and gave his work a proud nod before setting his focus back on Shepherd.

"Nutley is on-air as we speak," Shepherd said. He wiped newly formed beads of sweat from his head. "He's apologizing to the nation. He understands that what he said was wrong and that there are consequences for the things he says."

Joros took a deep breath and let it out slowly. "There is

an election in five days. I have been working on this election for a very long time--decades."

"I understand, sir, it's just--"

"Let me be clear," Joros said. "I am less than two weeks away from fundamentally transforming the United States of America."

"I understand," said Shepherd. "Polling data shows Democrats increasing their supermajority in the Senate and the president being re-elected easily. It's all but certain. This incident will have no bearing on that. I assure you the election is safe, sir."

Joros let the words sink in. Four years of Democrat rule had brought change to the country, but not enough change. He was close, but his vision, he knew, could not be fully realized without another four years. All his money, his political ground troops, and his strategies and tactics had worked brilliantly so far. The moment of total control was finally within reach.

He turned to the men at the door.

One of them stepped forward and set a black briefcase on the table, then returned to his post.

Joros lifted the case's cover, exposing tight, neat bundles of one-thousand dollar bills. "This is on top of what we have already agreed upon. Consider it an added incentive. I want to see a big push the rest of the way."

"Of course, this is very generous, as always," Shepherd said. He hesitated and seemed to be grasping for words.

"Something is not right?" Joros asked.

"This thing with Nutley. It makes me wonder if maybe some of our people could come off message."

"What do you mean?"

Shepherd sighed. "Lately, even our seasoned veterans seem to be having a hard time keeping themselves together. I think it's the president. They're absolutely smitten with him. They lose control at the mere mention of his name."

"Yes, I've noticed."

"It's just something to keep in the back of our minds," Shepherd said.

"That's why I pay you. To keep things in the back of your mind."

"Yes, sir. I just want to make sure we have the right expectations for our newscasters and reporters. We might not be able to control them forever."

"I don't need forever. I just need two more weeks. I can trust you to keep your people in line for two weeks?"

"Yes," Shepherd said. "Of course."

"But it is a shame about Nutley," Joros said. "He has always been so loyal. It's why I chose to give him the Brightman truth serum video."

"And he did a wonderful job with it. It wrapped up that election for us. Without it, we may well have lost. That would have set us back years. And it has all but ended Brightman's career."

Joros nodded. "It's too bad Brightman won't be around much longer. He is a great villain for us."

He stood and walked toward the door. "Two more weeks," he said. "Keep your people in line."

***

Nutley knew from the onslaught of emails and the

brutality of the blogs that damage control was not going to be easy, but he was confident that he could put the issue behind him.

He walked through the newsroom with a quick "hi," "hey," or "how you doing?" to everyone he passed. In return, each coworker sent him a nasty sneer or a loathsome head shake--except the ones who completely ignored him. When he reached the set, Billy Sample, his usually energetic tech-savvy assistant, approached him.

"Glad to see you're not avoiding me too," Nutley said. "I know this is going to sound crazy, but I don't even know what I said. And no one will give me the time of day. Maybe you can pull the tapes later and we can go through them."

Billy held up a single sheet of paper, the prepared opening Nutley was given before every show, and dropped it in his boss' direction. The paper floated left and right in the air before gliding under a table where two staff writers sat, drinking coffee. Although both of the writers had watched the paper slide under the table, neither so much as pretended to make an effort for it.

Nutley gave Billy his deepest, disappointed expression.

Billy flipped open his phone, started a conversation, and walked away.

Nutley sighed. Even Billy hated him now. And Billy wasn't just his assistant, he was his apprentice, his protégé. Without Nutley in his corner, the kid might never get a shot at a journalist's gig, and he was obviously willing to give that up. If any proof was needed to highlight how bad Nutley had screwed up, that was it.

He turned his attention back to the slip of paper lying under the table. Pushing his gimpy, tingling leg far to the left, he struggled to work himself down to his hands and knees, crawled under the table, and grabbed the paper. After struggling back to his feet, he headed to the corner of the room where Suzie, his makeup artist, waited.

"Ready to make me beautiful?" Nutley said in a jestful tone as he sat in the swivel chair. "I mean handsome," he quickly corrected with a nervous grimace. "Not beautiful. Women are beautiful. Men are handsome. Manly, and handsome, and straight."

Without saying a word, Suzie made a quick job of applying blush to Nutley's cheeks and then moved on, with a severe lack of motivation, to his hair.

As Suzie worked, Nutley turned his attention to the paper with the scripted opening. He scanned the first few sentences of the apology, then crumpled the paper into a ball and tossed it onto the counter. This needed to be in his own words, from the heart, and he knew exactly what he wanted to say.

The show's director came over to the makeup area. He ignored Nutley as he spoke. "Almost done, Suzie? One minute to air time."

Nutley pushed himself out of the chair and made his way toward the set.

"Hey, Nutley," someone behind him said, finally violating the company-wide silent treatment. "Nice work yesterday."

Nutley knew the voice immediately. "Thanks, Maddle," he said, turning toward the newcomer. "I'd like to stay and chat but I have a number one show to get to." He smiled to rub in his ratings dominance as he continued walking.

"We'll just have to see what kind of hit you take from Halendros-gate," Maddle called.

As he took his seat on the set, Nutley felt as though he sank through the floor--a ratings hit would be devastating. He couldn't allow it. Starting right now, he needed to be at the top of his game.

"Four, three, two." The cameraman pointed to Nutley with his middle finger as the "On Air" sign lit up.

"Good afternoon," Nutley said into the camera. He took a deep, slow, dramatic breath. "Before we start tonight, I want to take a few moments to speak about what happened yesterday.

"Let me be clear. There is no place in civil discourse for what was said on this show. As a society, we must be able to understand the difference between good and evil. When we fail to understand that difference, and we treat good and evil on par with each other, we are doing a tremendous disservice to the country.

"The man I had on my show, Natanio Halendros, is the antithesis of everything that we, in a civilized society, stand for. He is the evil that we must recognize. His views and beliefs are not only archaic and narrow-minded, but his words are inflammatory. He is horrible, rotten man."

Nutley cleared his throat and took a sip of water from the glass that sat on the table.

"When I unintentionally agreed with one of his ideas it was a serious, but very temporary, lapse in judgment. Make no mistake, affording civility to a man like that is like congratulating a thief or praising a killer. Worse. At least we have laws to deal with thieves and killers. But we have nothing to curb the hatred spewed by terrible men like him.

"Comments, such as the ones I made yesterday agreeing with that man, will never be made on this show again."

He looked over to the phone bank. Dozens of lights flashed. "Now, let's take a couple of calls."

Billy patched in the first one. The caller's name and location displayed on the screen at the front of the set.

"Stan from Marblehead, Massachusetts," Nutley said. "What's on your mind, Stan?"

"Merv, I heard your apology and I have to be honest. I don't know if it's good enough for me. That man you had on your show is a Goddamn prick. Can I say that on the air?"

"I think in this case we can allow it."

"Well that's what he is, and you treated him like he was royalty or something. You're supposed to know better than that."

"Well, I do," Nutley said. "No one is more upset at the way I acted than I am. Trust me, nobody understands the pure evil of these people as much as I do. Maybe we should take a moment to talk about how these kinds of people should be treated."

Suddenly, the phone disconnected and the "On Air" light turned off. Puzzled, Nutley checked the clock on the far wall. Six minutes remained in the opening segment.

Shepherd, who rarely appeared on set, stood off to the side. The CEO pointed toward Nutley as he whispered to the show's producer.

"What's going on?" Nutley said as he left the set and approached Shepherd.

Shepherd looked past Nutley like he wasn't there.

"Maddle. You're on."

Maddle got comfortable in the chair on Nutley's set.

"That's my chair," Nutley said. "That's my set. "What are you doing?"

"You're fired," Shepherd said before walking away.

Fired? That was impossible. He had the highest rated show in his time slot. "This is a joke, right?" he called to his boss as Maddle began the next segment.

"Good evening, everyone. I'm Pat Maddle. I will be with you in this time slot for now on and you can feel assured that I know what is appropriate to say and what is not. Tonight, we'll discuss how our president is fighting for you with winning policies and steadfast leadership."

The image on screen changed to one of President Puppit.

The instant Puppit's image appeared on the screen, Nutley's left leg tingled. He tried to ignore it as he shuffled off after Shepherd, but his leg went numb and he tumbled to the floor.

CHAPTER 4

In the darkness, Dr. Albert Gress nervously scanned the street, double checking that no one else was around. The late October evening air added to the goose bumps already on his arms.

"Psst, Troller," he whispered, leaning around the corner of a brick building.

Senator Troller's eyes darted left, then right, scanning the alleyway. His head remained still--perhaps intentionally, perhaps due to the limited range of motion from his short, fat neck.

After spotting the doctor, he started his approach. Bottom heavy, potbellied, and just under five feet tall, the Democrat senator moved slowly. Breathing heavily, he arrived in front of the doctor.

Gress grinned. Troller was a vision of beauty. Yellow gapped teeth, sparse wispy hair, and pocked, blotched skin adorned his primeval bone structure. If ever there was a man who would appreciate the doctor's life work, it was the physical anomaly that stood before him.

"What?" Troller said abruptly. His voice was raspy and his halitosis severe. He sniffled, then wiped his nose on his sleeve.

"Senator," the doctor said, "I have a proposition that might interest you."

"Mm-hmm," Troller said without emotion.

"I've developed some potions--elixirs, medicines, what

have you." The doctor leaned down and whispered into Troller's ear. "The tiniest amount of my potion, a drop the size of a pinhead, will turn any man into a specimen of genetic perfection."

Troller's eyes beamed. "Really?" He paused for a moment, then squinted. "Why should I believe this?"

"I am living proof," Gress said. "You are looking at a man who has benefited from these very potions." He pulled a photograph out of his pocket and handed it to Troller. "Not long ago, I was shorter, heavier, and balder than I am today."

Troller pulled a pair of glasses from his shirt pocket and rested them on the bridge of his thick nose. He glanced from the photo, to Gress, and back to the photo again.

"I was not born with the magnificent bone structure you see here," Gress said, waving his hand to showcase his handsome face. "Nor this perfect head of hair." He ran his fingers through his thick, black locks. "Nor this physique." He stood tall, puffing out his chest.

Truly proud of his work, Gress loved showing it off. It had started with years of studying and researching human genetic structure. That was followed by a decade of collecting the finest samples of DNA from living genetic studs as well as descendants of admired greatness--from politicians to scientists to athletes. Much of it, of course, was grunt work in the form of countless nights digging through graveyards and collecting tissue samples that would be otherwise unattainable. But the breakthrough, the real genius, was the process to purify and deliver, via his potions, the most desirable attributes of any gene. And now he sought the help of an evolutionary misfit to bring his crowning achievement to the masses.

"I don't believe it," Troller said, folding his glasses and putting them back in his pocket.

"Well, I am prepared to let you see for yourself." Gress pulled a half-dozen small glass vials from his coat pocket and held them in front of Troller. "You can grow hair, or clear your skin. You can improve your eyesight. Grow taller or more muscular."

Troller's eyes widened and the beginnings of a smile formed on his lips. He grabbed at the potions in Gress's hand.

"No," Gress said, raising the vials high above Troller's head as the senator jumped, but failed to reach them. "First, I need your help."

Troller stopped reaching for the potions and listened.

"Sodium," Gress said, "has been so highly regulated that I can no longer buy it in the quantities I need for my work."

An expression of pure confusion overtook Troller's face.

"Sodium is an essential ingredient in my potions," Gress said. "While the potions themselves only contain a modest amount, the development and testing requires vast amounts."

Troller stared stone faced at the doctor.

"Salt," Gress continued. "You and your colleagues have made it all but impossible for me to acquire it in the amounts I need. I want you to use your influence in the Senate so I can get around the regulations that limit me."

"And if I help?"

"Then you would be like my partner, and I would cut you in for a percentage of the profits."

Troller blinked slowly.

"Think about it," Gress said. "You would get a percentage of the greatest, most profitable invention in human history." He put the vials back in his pocket. "It will make you a very rich man."

A full smile worked its way onto Troller's face.

Gress was not interested in the money for himself. He had a less superficial motivation: to make the human race better by weeding out all of the genetic shortcomings that had so unfortunately plagued man for all of history. His work would be the beginning of human perfection.

Troller eyed the doctor's pocket. His nostrils flared as he pointed to it. "Hand them over."

"Quiet," Gress said, looking around to make sure Troller hadn't called attention to them. "Now that I have your interest, let's get off this street and find a more private place to talk. My lab, perhaps."

Troller sneered and grunted. He took a half-step forward and kicked the doctor between the legs.

Pain shot up Gress's stomach. He doubled over, clutching his groin, and let out a wincing groan.

Troller lunged forward, knocking over and smothering his victim with all two-hundred plump pounds of himself.

Blanketed by Troller's torso, Gress fought to turn his head and allow a path of air to his mouth. With one giant heave, he pushed his attacker off, rolling him to the side.

Troller worked himself to a standing position and waddled hurriedly down the alley.

Gress got to his knees. He reached into his jacket pocket and pulled out two empty vials--but no full ones. Troller had stolen all of his valid samples.

Staggering and hunched over, he chased the Democrat to the end of the alley where Troller hailed a taxi. "Get back here," Gress called.

The cab screeched to a stop. Gress lunged forward in an effort to grab the senator before he got in, but a man turning the corner got in the way and collided with the doctor.

Gress disentangled himself from the stranger. Still doubled over in pain, he hobbled along the sidewalk, following the cab. "Senator, please. You must know what you are doing with those."

***

Nutley shuffled lazily along the streets of downtown Washington, D.C. His head hung low, his pride lower. For so long, he had been on top of his game, on top of the media world. For so long, he could do no wrong. Now, it seemed, he could do no right.

When he finally lifted his head, the sun had dropped to the horizon. He found himself gazing across the Lincoln Memorial Reflecting Pool to the Washington Monument.

The evening chill struck through his shirt.

He shivered, buttoned his coat, and dropped himself onto a bench. His eyes glazed over, fixated on the tall obelisk. His leg tingled. He rubbed it. The damn leg. What could he do about it? No doctor had offered so much as a guess except Schwartz.

Nutley laughed to himself as he considered the doctor's inane diagnosis. The doctor's entire way of thinking was ridiculous. He didn't need to confront anything. What he needed to do was forget about it. Push it aside and ignore it.

After all, if he hadn't been so focused on his leg while interviewing Halendros, he would still have his job. Yes, the way to get through this was to put it out of his mind. Besides, a dozen doctors had agreed he was otherwise healthy. He was making too much of this. It was time to focus on more important things, like getting his show back.

He could do it. He could get back on top. Maddle had no experience, but Nutley had broken hundreds of stories. Broken a few careers as well. As he cycled through his accomplishments in his mind, a new vigor arose in him. He could do it. But to be top dog, leaning down to sneer at Maddle, he needed to give Shepherd what he wanted. A story. A big story.

He grinned, shame and anger put aside by his new decision. One thing he was sure of--in this town there was always a story. He would need to draw on his expertise and years of experience. Big stories like the one he needed didn't just come crashing into you. Deep in thought, he turned the corner.

A bone-rattling crunch knocked him backward. Dazed, and through blurry eyes, he squinted to focus on the man who just crashed into him.

"Senator, please," the silhouetted man yelled as he ran, hunched over, along the sidewalk. "You must know what you are doing with those."

Nutley peered down the block at the man chasing the speeding cab, then shook his head, still adjusting from the collision. Looking down, he noticed the man had dropped some belongings. He gathered two small glass vials from the ground.

Having learned from his early days on the beat to save anything and everything, he put the items in his coat pocket. Old napkins, discarded mail, a cigar--you never knew when the most insignificant object might lead to a scoop. He stood for a moment as the idea of a big-time, breakout story percolated in his head. Then, something else grabbed his attention--*Senator*.

That man was chasing a senator. He was robbed, maybe attacked, by a senator. Nutley smiled. Something just went down. He didn't know what, exactly, but it had all the makings of a big story. The kind of story he needed. He peered along the quiet street and down the empty alley. He was the only one in the know. He clenched his fist in excitement as questions raced through his mind. What kind of senator would blatantly steal and attack? Easy. A Republican. But would a Republican even be that brazen? Probably. Definitely, if he didn't care about re-election. His mind churned, putting two and two together. A minute later, he had his answer. He let it simmer in his head. No. It couldn't be. He added it up again. Yes.

Brightman.

It had to be Brightman. A story of a typical senator's scandal had no legs, no staying power. It was far too common an occurrence. But a scandal with Brightman was altogether different.

An excited laugh bubbled up from his gut. This couldn't have worked out better if he planned it himself. Shepherd would love it. His audience would eat it up. If he could nail Brightman like he did four years ago, he'd be back on top to stay.

***

After pushing this week's pile of pornographic magazines off the end of his bed, Senator Troller set down the vials.

With his long, dirty fingernails, he pried the cap off the first vial. A tentative whiff revealed no obvious smell. He put his tongue on the container's opening and flipped it up, allowing a single drop of the slightly salty liquid to slip into his mouth. He re-capped the small bottle and waited, concentrating to feel any changes coming.

One by one, he opened the remaining containers, took a tiny sip, closed it, and waited for something to happen. As he popped the top off the last vial, his eyes grew heavy. He struggled to put the final drop in his mouth, then capped the vial before falling backwards onto his bed.

Dull, painless pangs ran across his body in all directions, massaging and vibrating him from the inside. He remained still for a moment, enjoying the strange feeling as he drifted off to sleep.

When he woke, he lay on his back, mesmerized by the image staring down at him from the full-length mirror on the ceiling above his bed.

Who was this man looking back at him? He lifted his right arm off the bed. The man in the mirror lifted his left. He lifted his left arm, and the man looking back moved his right.

He studied the reflection above, in awe of the thick wavy hair, broad shoulders, and large frame that allowed his feet to extend beyond the mattress. A flutter of butterflies danced in his stomach.

Realizing his clothes had ripped at the seams from his

new physique, he sat up and finished the job, tearing them off down to his briefs and socks, and then made his way to the bathroom to get a better look at himself.

The butterflies danced again. This time, behind a ripped six-pack.

He inspected his face, slowly running his hands around it, caressing every inch. His cheekbones were high, his jaw strong. He smiled and gawked at himself. Brilliant white teeth glistened. The new him did not disappoint. He was fantastic.

With flexed biceps, the once beastly, now becoming senator held his arms high and studied his bulging veins. He twisted to a side view, extended his arms downward, and marveled at his triceps. He stuck out his chest and examined its musculature. For the next hour, he admired his beauty in every pose to which he could contort his body.

Grabbing a magazine from the counter and holding it at arm's length, he compared himself to the teen model on the cover. He threw the magazine down and raised his arms in victory. It was time to introduce the world to the Troller it had never seen. With his newfound beauty, women would adore him. The country would admire him. His colleagues, the very men who mocked and snickered at him in private and in public, would envy him.

He rummaged through his drawers for clothes to fit his tall, buff body, but his old shirts and pants would simply not stretch enough.

As he searched for more clothes, he glanced at the vials on the bed. He didn't need them anymore, and he certainly didn't want anyone else getting their hands on them. He brought them into the bathroom, opened them, and poured them down the sink.

As the liquids mixed, they sizzled, flowing down the drain. Gurgling ensued, followed by knocking. In a flash, a plume of thick black smoke exploded from the sink, throwing the gorgeous senator backwards.

Gagging and coughing, he lost his balance and fell to the floor as the heavy smoke blanketed the room.

He crawled into the living room in search of clean air. His eyes teared and his head pounded. His lungs filled with the grit that hung in the air and wads of phlegm splattered on the floor from his violent coughs. He collapsed onto his stomach, rolled onto his back, and clutched his head. When he opened his mouth to scream, he could only cough and gag. He remained still, hoping for the nightmare to end.

But new pains came. Shooting pains. They started at his head and blasted to his toes. Others followed, burning a path from his chest to his fingertips, accompanied by a crackling sound that electrified the air.

Fighting through the agony, he struggled to his feet-- and banged his head against the ceiling as he stood upright. He ducked under the doorway into the bathroom, then wiped a layer of black ash off the mirror. Hunching over, he peered into it.

His mouth dropped. His breath vanished. The man staring back at him was as horrid a sight as he had ever seen. His short-lived, Adonis-like beauty now corrupted by a fusion of disfigured facial features. Every unfortunate, physical characteristic Troller had despised about himself was now intensified and magnified. And, in addition to the hideousness of his face, he now stood, by his estimation, about twelve feet tall.

Without warning, the shooting pains returned and his body convulsed. His arms and legs grew.

The pains returned again. And again. Each time, he watched in horror as his limbs ripped and stretched.

In a matter of minutes, he was too big for the small room. Like a caged animal, he attacked his surroundings, clawing to free himself. He flung his arms and kicked his legs, breaking through the plaster on the walls. With a roar, he forced his way through the front door, ripping it from its hinges. He lumbered, hunched over, down the hallway. Pictures flew off the wall and ceiling lights popped as he squeezed his ever-growing body out of the building.

It was before dawn. A slight mist, plus the seasonably brisk weather, ensured the streets were empty.

Standing in front of his apartment building, he rested his hands on the top of an SUV and braced for more agonizing growth.

It came. Again and again.

When, finally, some minutes had passed with no more change, he stood upright, at eye level with the roof of the five-story building, his privacy covered only by the frayed briefs that clung to his waist by threads.

He held his arms out at length, examining their enormous size, trying to understand what he had become. Women would not adore him. The country would not admire him. His colleagues would not envy him.

His colossal rage matched his massive body. He raised his arms and sent them barreling down on the roof of the SUV in front of him.

The sound of crushing metal rang through the night air as the truck crumbled from the force.

He bent down to get a closer look at the damage he caused. He smiled. A sense of satisfaction soothed him.

CHAPTER 5

When Brightman had the opportunity to give elementary school kids a tour of the Capitol, he fully expected it to be the only enjoyable time of his day. He always looked forward to sharing his passion--his country's history, founding, and ideals--with anyone who had not yet soured on him from the personal attacks carted out by the media over the last few years.

He met Mrs. Appleton, the fourth-grade teacher, in the hallway just outside the Capitol and then introduced himself to the fifty or so students that stood before him. He pushed open the large oak door and motioned for everyone to follow as he walked to the center of the room.

"The room we are standing in, the Rotunda, is the most recognizable part of this building. Its brilliance starts at the top of the dome, 180 feet up, where you will see The Apotheosis of Washington, a fresco painting by Constantino Brumidi, and it reaches to a room below us, known as the Crypt, which was designed as the final resting place for George Washington's tomb.

"Now, if you look around the walls, you'll notice eight historic oil paintings and a number of statues. All of these--"

The doors from the Senate wing swung open. Two men entered, one tall and thin, the other short and portly. The tap of their footsteps on the marble floor carried through the air.

"And here are some more of your senators now," Brightman said. "They are part of the committee you'll be watching in the gallery later."

As the senators approached Mrs. Appleton and introduced themselves, a deep rumble shook the building, interrupting the salutations.

"Is this an earthquake?" Mrs. Appleton said, opening her arms wide in a gesture to gather and protect the children.

Another rumble, significantly louder, shook the building again. Bits of plaster from the ceiling's fresco artwork rained down.

"Let's get outside," Brightman said. He turned toward the door but a huge shockwave sent him reeling back. He stumbled as a number of children fell to the floor.

As everyone got back on their feet and rushed to escape, a fracture formed at the bottom of the front wall and zigzagged upwards. Chunks of sandstone shot out as the crack picked up speed and reached the ceiling. With a high-pitched creak, a large section of the cast iron dome dislodged and fell. It crashed to the ground, opening a ten-foot-wide crater in the center of the floor, and blocking the path to the doors.

The building shook again and the children--and the two Democrat senators--screamed in panic as they dodged the debris that continued to fall.

An explosion rocked the front wall. Twenty feet up from the ground, a tree-trunk-sized projectile punched its way through, sending fragments rocketing across the room. Another section exploded as the projectile plowed through again. It seemed impossible, but they appeared to be giant fists.

Another rumble sounded--a prolonged one that grew louder and gained strength. The louder it got, the more the building shook.

The front wall crumbled.

A blinding blanket of smoke and dust poured into the air. It swirled, clearing slightly as a hideous fifty-foot-tall monster stepped through the gaping hole.

***

Joros slashed a red line across the paper to strike out yet another sentence but the line faded halfway to the edge of the sheet. He touched the felt tip to his tongue, slightly wetting it, and tried again before tossing the empty marker in the trash.

He rubbed his eyes, leaned back, and fingered through the stack of papers sitting in the corner of his desk. They overflowed with edits. Rewriting a constitution was indeed a lot of work, and he was anxious to have it ready when his Democrats swept the upcoming election.

He pondered what this election meant. Change. He would finally create the change he had worked toward for so long. He thought of the countless times his efforts had run into a wall over the last three years. It was a wall more than two centuries old and made of parchment, but proving to be as unshakable as solid concrete.

There had been some successes, of course. But in each case the change only went so far. By the time this election was over, the polls told him, he would control three-fourths of the state legislatures and two-thirds of the Congress and

Senate. Then, he could ratify anything. It was the light at the end of this tunnel that kept him going.

For now, though, he needed a break. He pulled the belt on his velvet robe, spun his chair to the television mounted on the wall behind him, and clicked it on with the remote.

His heart fluttered when he saw the images on the screen and he leaned forward, engrossing himself in the live footage of a massive creature wreaking havoc along the streets of D.C. He shrieked with pleasure as the giant tore through the wall on the Capitol Rotunda. "Isn't this just fantastic?" he said, leaping from his chair.

He immediately composed himself, checked the room to make sure he was alone, adjusted his robe, and sat himself down again.

The scenes on the television were stunning, true, but he mustn't get carried away. With the election only a few days away, an unplanned crisis like this had the potential to gum up the works. He needed to know what was going on. Who or what was this creature? And where did it come from?

He dialed Shepherd on his cell. "What is going on?"

"We aren't completely sure yet, sir."

"Find out and call me back."

He flipped his phone closed and turned his attention back to the screen. His nerves unsettled as the possible complications to his plans played out in his mind. He had to get in front of this story. He had to use this to his advantage.

***

*** BREAKING NEWS ***

*** CARRI CARRINGTON, ROB ROBERTS REPORTING ***

*** BEGIN OFFICIAL TRANSCRIPT ***

CARRI CARRINGTON: I'm Carri Carrington.

ROB ROBERTS: And I'm Rob Roberts, reporting from Washington, D.C. with breaking news.

CARRI CARRINGTON: A Republican is destroying the city.

ROB ROBERTS: A fifty-foot giant creature-- you heard that right--a giant is attacking our capitol city.

CARRI CARRINGTON: Unspecified sources have confirmed the Republican Party is behind it.

ROB ROBERTS: Is it some sort of monster the Republicans ginned up?

CARRI CARRINGTON: Is it an actual Republican?

ROB ROBERTS: We just don't know yet.

CARRI CARRINGTON: But what we do know is that this Republican plan to destroy the city is having devastating effects.

ROB ROBERTS: We have Phil Phillips joining us live from ground zero. Phil, how bad is it?

PHIL PHILLIPS, CORRESPONDENT: It's pretty bad, Rob. I'm at the intersection of Massachusetts and New York avenues and you can see here that the giant came up this way along Massachusetts Ave. and the destruction, I mean, it's just hard to imagine--overturned cars, toppled buildings, power lines are down.

In fact, if you look here to the left, this space between these buildings, well, it wasn't there earlier. There was actually an apartment building there and it has been simply pulverized. It's just a big hole where there used to be an entire building.

CARRI CARRINGTON: My God. How tragic. Let me ask you Phil, did poor people live there?

PHIL PHILLIPS: Poor people? I don't believe so.

ROB ROBERTS: I see. What about black people?

PHIL PHILLIPS: Um, I'm really not sure.

CARRI CARRINGTON: How about old people, Phil? Any old people live there?

PHIL PHILLIPS: You know, I don't--

ROB ROBERTS: Any cripples?

PHIL PHILLIPS: As far as I know it was just a regular apartment building.

CARRI CARRINGTON: Oh.

ROB ROBERTS: Oh. Well. Still a terrible thing. Silly question, Phil, but the giant isn't there now?

PHIL PHILLIPS: No. I was talking to some people a few minutes ago and he seems to have worked his way south down 395. I haven't seen it myself but, from what I understand, the highway is a mess. I would certainly caution anyone from getting on these roads.

ROB ROBERTS: Phil, if you take 395 south from where you are, that's a low income area, I believe. Can you confirm that the giant Republican has, in fact, headed toward an area with a lot of poor people? Preferably poor minorities.

PHIL PHILLIPS: I'm not all that familiar--

ROB ROBERTS: What about a dog run? A nursing home?

CARRI CARRINGTON: Oh, I got one, what about an orphanage?

ROB ROBERTS: Oh, yes, good, an orphanage. Phil, what do you think? Maybe we have an orphanage there?

PHIL PHILLIPS: Um, I'm going to have to get back to you on that.

CARRI CARRINGTON: Okay, well, we'll keep our fingers crossed.

ROB ROBERTS: Hold on. I'm getting word that the giant has made his way to the U.S. Capitol. We've got a camera nearby. Let's take a look. Phil, thanks, we're going to cut you loose now. But check on that orphanage and get back to us.

(BEGIN VIDEO)

ROB ROBERTS (VOICEOVER): And there he is.

CARRI CARRINGTON (VOICEOVER): My God he is disgusting. Just hideous.

ROB ROBERTS (VOICEOVER): And it appears he is approaching the Capitol and--oh boy-- there he goes. Right through the wall of the Capitol.

(STATIC ON VIDEO, VIDEO FEED LOST)

CARRI CARRINGTON: Wow. Well, it seems we've lost our live feed from the Capitol. I don't know that there are words for this. Simply stunning.

ROB ROBERTS: Okay, I think the question on everyone's mind is: Why? Why would the Republicans do this?

CARRI CARRINGTON: Because they're a-holes.

ROB ROBERTS: Still, this seems a bit extreme. On the bright side, this disaster can serve as a wake-up call for Election Day to anyone who was not planning on voting Democrat. So let's make sure we all get out there and pull the lever for President Obie Puppit. We need (INAUDIBLE GURGLING, GAGGING, AND DROOLING).

CARRI CARRINGTON: Oh my God. You're slobbering again.

ROB ROBERTS: I'm sorry. (INAUDIBLE GURGLING) There's no diagnosis for this yet. Just can't seem to (INAUDIBLE GAGGING) no matter how much I swallow. Can I get somebody over here to wipe this up?

CARRI CARRINGTON: No one wants to touch

that. You know what, can I get someone here to actually report the news without drooling all over me every newscast?

ROB ROBERTS: Don't flatter yourself, I'm not drooling all over you.

CARRI CARRINGTON: You're drooling all over pretty much everything in sight for the past four years and it's--you know what, let's just get back to the news.

ROB ROBERTS: Like I was saying, President Puppit (INAUDIBLE GURGLING)

CARRI CARRINGTON: Uhg. Just so gross. Look at you. It's dripping down your chin. You're like a Republican.

*** END TRANSCRIPT ***

***

The giant scratched his fat hanging belly and stepped inside the building. He dropped to one knee, raised his hands, and brought them smashing down, pounding the ground and sending shockwaves through the room.

"Get over here," Blumble said, grabbing the largest fourth-grader of the group and cowering behind the child.

Cratt yanked the kid by the shirt, trying to pull him away from Blumble.

"Get your own," Blumble said, reaching for a second, and then a third student.

"You're taking all the big ones," Cratt said, pulling harder on the young boy's shirt until the collar ripped off. "I'm the senior guy here."

As Blumble secured the three children in front of him and backpedaled to the wall, Cratt nabbed a fleeing girl. Her legs flailed in the air as he lifted her close to his chest, but the petite crying child provided little cover for the robust senator. He tossed her to the side and latched on to Mrs. Appleton.

Brightman spotted a large splintered piece of wood on the ground. He picked it up and flung it at the giant. It flew, end over end, and stuck into the top of the giant's foot. The monster became distracted as he hesitated and inspected it.

"Run," Brightman shouted. "Hurry!"

Blumble and Cratt flung their human shields aside, sending them flying across the floor. The Democrats stumbled as they fled for the exit, fighting each other to be the first one out.

Brightman helped Mrs. Appleton to her feet, then the two of them ushered the children out. When the students were all gone, Brightman nudged the teacher out the door after them.

The giant pulled the splinter out of his foot and tossed it aside. He moved forward, cutting off Brightman's path to the exit.

Alone in the room with the monster, Brightman looked left, then right. There was no escape. He pushed his back up against the wall and braced for the creature's next move.

As the giant stepped forward, his foot fell through the crater in the floor. Undistracted, he shook his leg, pulled it out, and continued.

Brightman glanced at the hole. It was his only way out. He sprinted toward it. But the giant's massive hand swung down, plowing into the senator's side and launching him into the air. He landed with a belly flop, bounced, tumbled, and slid to a stop. He scampered to his feet and raced again to the hole in the middle of the room.

The giant slapped at his prey and Brightman dodged the enormous fingers flying at him. He dove into the crater, landing with a breath-stealing thud on the Crypt floor below.

Dazed, he rolled onto his back and looked up to find the giant staring down at him. He staggered to his feet and raced along the underground corridor to a metal staircase that led outside to the front lawn.

The Rotunda lay in shambles. The giant stood in the middle of the rubble and roared. Deafening sound waves rocked the ground and rattled trees. He swung his enormous arms at the remaining portions of the walls, shattering them and filling the air with a tsunami of debris. A piercing creak emanated from what remained of the dome. It tilted, then fell, and a massive plume of smoke rose as the cast iron structure crashed to the ground.

Brightman scanned the area, searching for a way to get the giant out of the city and as far away as possible.

A school bus sat parked across the lawn. He raced to it, turned the key, revved the engine, and jammed the gas pedal hard to the floor.

The bus shot forward, toward the Capitol steps. It crashed into the bottom step with full force, then struggled for traction as the wheels slipped, slowly climbing to the top.

Leaning on the horn, Brightman headed straight toward the gaping hole in the wall. He slammed on the brakes. The tires screeched as the bus stopped a dozen yards from the giant.

The monster turned and stopped pounding, mesmerized by the bright yellow.

Brightman spun the bus and floored the gas pedal. He headed back to the steps and bounded down onto the front lawn, then shifted into high gear and flew down Pennsylvania Ave.

The giant, only a hundred feet back, paced him perfectly, the boom of each earth-shattering step temporarily muting the screaming engine.

Brightman grabbed the steering wheel tight. His plan was simple. Once he got to the interstate, he would take it north to some desolate farmland. The half-full tank of gas would last him an hour, maybe two.

His mind flashed with memories from his days in a fighter jet. If he were behind the controls of an FT-15, he would lock-in and send two streaming missiles, one from each wing, to destroy his target. But instead, he sat behind the controls of a yellow school bus.

Ahead, a stop light turned red. A compact hybrid, crossing the intersection, putted along.

Brightman blared the horn repeatedly as he flew closer to the intersection. "Out of the way!" He leaned on the horn hard. "Move!"

He reached the intersection with the compact dead ahead.

He swerved left.

The tires screamed and the bus fishtailed.

He spun the steering wheel hard right.

The bus fell on its side with a crash. It skidded,

grinding across the pavement.

Brightman clutched the wheel and braced his feet on the floor as rocks and sparks shot through the broken window, pelting him in the face as the bus scraped along the asphalt, back end first, into a row of storefronts. Shattering glass echoed.

When the bus grinded to a halt, there was silence. No crashing. No cracking. No thunderous booms from giant footsteps.

Disoriented, Brightman turned himself to get a read on his location. Black pavement sat just out the window to his left. The blue morning sky shined through the doors to his right.

A moment later, the giant's head eclipsed the sunlit sky. The creature stood above, straddling the vehicle.

Brightman pulled the lever to open the door. It didn't budge. He braced himself and kicked it with both feet, but the metal frame didn't give an inch.

As the giant's mammoth hands clasped the front end of the bus, Brightman scampered over the seats, trying to reach the rear. He tumbled to the back, crashing into the emergency door as the bus was lifted off the ground. He pounded the door until flew open, and he fell to the pavement.

The giant brought the bus to eye level. He peered inside, then shook it violently. Chips of glass rained down and he tossed the bus aside, landing it with a crash on the rooftop of a nearby building. Leaning forward, he scanned the area and spotted Brightman.

Brightman jumped to his feet and fled but the giant reached down and wrapped his large fingers around the senator. His grip tightened as he lifted his prize.

CHAPTER 6

As Joros stared at the television screen, admiring the monstrous creature's work, something unexpected caught his attention. He rewound the footage ten seconds, then went forward in slow motion to see the giant running down Pennsylvania Avenue frame by frame.

When a clear image of the giant, from behind, settled on the screen, he paused the action. He zoomed in on the image, heading straight for the giant's rear--his left cheek, specifically.

There it was. The mark. Clear as day: D.U.M.I.

The giant was one of his senators.

He clenched both fists and pounded on his desk. Just days before a landslide victory, and one of them goes off and does something stupid. "Come in here," he said into the intercom.

Two men in black suits entered.

"He is one of mine," Joros said, pointing to the television. "Find out which one."

The two men nodded and left the room. They returned a few minutes later. "We've located everyone but Troller."

"Bring him to me."

The men looked at each other, then to their boss. "But, he must be fifty feet tall. How? What--"

"Just tell him to come to me," Joros said calmly. "He will come."

An unsure look overcame the two men. "Yes, sir," they said unconfidently before leaving the room.

Joros leaned his head back and imagined what it could mean to harness the giant Democrat's power and unleash it strategically. He envisioned the senator running rampant, from coast to coast, pulverizing everything in sight.

***

Brightman pounded on the enormous fingers wrapped tightly around him. He grimaced and groaned, gasping for air.

The giant pulled him close, face to face, eye to basketball-sized eye, and let out a deafening roar. His hot, damp breath crashed against Brightman.

Streams of condensation formed instantly and dripped down the senator's face. He gagged and heaved, forcing out the little air that remained in his lungs.

The giant hung his mouth open. His teeth were discolored and diseased, but more than capable of tearing a man in half. He eased his prey toward the vast chasm.

As Brightman neared the opening, he reached up. With both hands, he grabbed the giant's upper lip, squeezed tight, twisted, and pinched.

The giant shot his head back and yelped, then placed his other hand on top of Brightman's shoulders, fully securing the senator in all ten of his tremendous fingers.

Brightman tensed every muscle as the giant lifted him back toward his massive mouth. He clenched his eyes, waiting for the inevitable.

But a whirring sounded in the distance and the giant, suddenly distracted, turned his head as a helicopter approached.

"Finally," Brightman, dizzy from lack of oxygen, "the cavalry." Through a flurry of stars in his vision, he strained to see the emblem on the sides of the copter. Navy? Air Force? But there was nothing to identify them.

A man leaned out of the chopper with a megaphone. "The boss wants you. Come."

The giant dropped his hands to his sides, loosening his grip as he focused on the helicopter.

Brightman sucked in a lungful of air, then squirmed and wiggled himself out of the giant's hand. He jumped to a strand of the creature's shredded underwear, gripped it tight, and shimmied his way down as far as he could go. He dropped the remaining distance to the ground and scrambled behind a flipped car.

The helicopter turned and flew away, and the giant followed, lumbering down the middle of the road, his every footstep sending shockwaves along the ground.

As Brightman watched the giant follow the helicopter, two questions hung in his mind. Where did he come from? And who had just taken him away?

He settled on the only answer he could imagine. A military experiment gone horribly wrong. An initiative, likely mishandled and neglected like everything else under the current administration, had fallen into irresponsible hands. But even this didn't provide all the answers. Someone had taken this giant away and, with the passing of NAMCA, he knew it wasn't the military.

With his gaze still fixed down the road, the questions

in his mind subsided. He felt something he hadn't felt in years. He felt needed. There were ninety-nine other senators in the Capitol, yet he was the only one to take action. Maybe the people he served didn't even realize they needed him, but, at this moment, he knew they did.

Two men cautiously stepped out from a shattered storefront and poked their heads around.

"It's gone," Brightman said. "Come on out."

The men came to the sidewalk. The younger man, a giant in his own right at about six foot six, focused on his cell phone. The older man, who seemed to be the father, turned back to the decimated storefront. He opened his arms wide and choked back tears as he spoke. "I built this. I spent my life building this business."

From a teetering door frame, an electric sign dangled at the end of two wires: "Carson's Uniforms & Costumes." The wires shorted, the fluorescent lights fluttered and sizzled, and a small cloud of black smoke puffed out before the wires snapped and the sign fell to the ground and shattered.

"Are you Carson?" Brightman asked in a consoling tone.

The man nodded slowly, unable to pull his misty eyes off his destroyed store. Another sign, "Open 24 Hours Through Halloween," was now the only thing that still hung in the tattered frame.

Brightman put his hand on the old man's shoulder but said nothing, respecting the silence that hung in the air.

"They're saying it was a giant Republican," the young man said, looking up from his phone.

Brightman rolled his eyes. "Don't believe everything you hear."

"Why would they do this?" the old man said, losing the

fight with his tears and erupting into hysterics.

The younger Carson squared his hulking shoulders toward Brightman. "You're a Republican, aren't you?"

Something told Brightman this man wasn't a partisan ally. He remained silent. This wasn't the time to argue politics and, judging by the size of the man, he wasn't the one to argue with.

"Yeah, you're Brightman," the big man said. "I remember when you ran for president. We voted for the other guy." He spit at the ground, never taking his eyes off the senator. "The other guy ain't a squealer."

The old man pulled away from Brightman's arm, stepping back and shooting an angry look at him.

More people came from the surrounding buildings and joined the scene. A few tentative stragglers at first, but soon a couple dozen onlookers crowded the small area, encircling Brightman and the two men from Carson's.

"Why don't you get out of here?" the old man said, wagging his finger in Brightman's face. "And don't come around again."

"Republicans," a woman from the crowd said, shaking her head.

"Figures," said someone else. "They'll destroy anything."

The bashing continued and the general anger was soon directed at Brightman.

"Why don't you just retire already?"

"I thought we got rid of you four years ago."

Brightman navigated through the crowd amid harsh stares, careful not to bump or knock anyone. He had two tours of duty under his belt, yet the unknown intentions of the crowd made him more uncomfortable than any enemy he had faced. In combat, the enemy hated you because they had to. These people hated him because they wanted to. When he reached the end of the crowd, the large young man stepped in front of him.

Brightman looked up at the menacing figure.

"Don't let me see you again, squealer. We don't need you and we don't want you."

Behind him, the crowd chimed in agreement.

***

*** BREAKING NEWS ***

*** MIKE MICHAELS REPORTING ***

*** BEGIN OFFICIAL TRANSCRIPT ***

MIKE MICHAELS: Hello everyone, I'm Mike Michaels reporting from just outside the Capitol. Or, more accurately, what was the Capitol until a few, short minutes ago. As you can see behind me, the Capitol is no more. Demolished. Destroyed, by a Republican monster.

But you'll also notice the monster is nowhere to be seen. Just moments ago, he left the Capitol in shambles and ran down the street, right down Pennsylvania Avenue, chasing a school bus. We don't yet know if there were any children on the bus.

I'm joined now by eye-witness and survivor of the calamity, Senator Joe Blumble of

Delaware. Senator Blumble was inside the Capitol when the Republican giant attacked and he came face to face with the monster. Senator, glad you're okay. Tell us what happened in there?

JOE BLUMBLE, DELAWARE SENATOR: You know, Mike, it's still all kind of a blur. I'm part of the, um, committee, the committee that, oh what the heck is it? Anyway, we were getting ready to meet and the thing just crashed through the wall. Just came crashing right through.

MIKE MICHAELS: Horrifying.

JOE BLUMBLE: F***ing-a-right it was.

MIKE MICHAELS: Whoa. Easy there, Senator.

JOE BLUMBLE: Oh, sorry about that. You can edit that out later, I'm sure.

MIKE MICHAELS: Um, no. This is live.

JOE BLUMBLE: You don't edit live coverage?

MIKE MICHAELS: Then it wouldn't be live.

JOE BLUMBLE: Okay, then.

MIKE MICHAELS: Back to the giant. Senator, what happened after he came crashing through the wall?

JOE BLUMBLE: A bunch of us banded together and went on offense.

MIKE MICHAELS: You did?

JOE BLUMBLE: Of course. Hey, there were kids in there. Some kind of a field trip or something was going on.

MIKE MICHAELS: So there were children in the Capitol when the giant attacked?

JOE BLUMBLE: Yes, indeed. Now, as a father, my first thought was "What if these kids have parents?"

MIKE MICHAELS: I'm guessing they probably do.

JOE BLUMBLE: Right. So, then they're part of a family. Good middle-class families, I bet. We stand up for the middle class. You gotta do what you can to protect them.

MIKE MICHAELS: I think what you mean is that you want to protect all children.

JOE BLUMBLE: Sure. So we got those kids out of there right away. Got them safe. Then we went to work on the giant. Went on offense. We punched and kicked, threw whatever we could find at it until it left.

MIKE MICHAELS: So Republicans create a monster that literally attacks children. Unbelievable. I guess they figure they don't have the votes to pass policy anymore and hurt the kids that way, so they try something like this.

Senator Blumble, you were face to face with this giant which makes you, really, the closest thing we have to an expert. Let me ask you, is this the work of moderate Republicans? Hard right wingers? I mean, what are we looking at here?

JOE BLUMBLE: Damned if I know. Ah sh**, I'm sorry about that again.

MIKE MICHAELS: It's okay. You can say "damned."

JOE BLUMBLE: I can?

MIKE MICHAELS: Yes, but you can't say the other one. The one that starts with "sh."

JOE BLUMBLE: Sh**? Oh, damn. Ah, f***.

MIKE MICHAELS: Hold on a second here. I'm getting word there has been an extraordinary event. The giant is gone. President Obie Puppit has gotten rid of the giant. Oh my goodness. Wow. Awesome. Amazing and unbelievable. You simply can't overestimate this guy. Just when you think he can't top himself, he single-handedly defeats the giant. Swatted him like a fly, I bet. Obviously, we're still waiting on betails here dut bis ib increbibub. Blorgog ug blenpum gribnab ogglebog greeg.

JOE BLUMBLE: You got that gibberish jaw again?

MIKE MICHAELS: (NODDING) Yaba baba. Glab dum dum.

JOE BLUMBLE: How long has that been happening to you, man?

MIKE MICHAELS: (HOLDING UP FOUR FINGERS) Yama obama mao mao.

JOE BLUMBLE: Three years. God bless you, man, that's a long time. Let me help you out here. Give me that microphone.

MIKE MICHAELS: No, I dink I'm dokay now. It's passed. I just get a dittle tongue tied scmetimes. Comes on real fast and real strong. Anyway, it seems President Obie Puppit has sabed the bay. Lorg knows how he bib it. Mayde he dim pumbleglub globajeep jig mabagago.

JOE BLUMBLE: Here, Mike, give me that microphone. Thanks. And the ear thing. Why don't you go over there? Sit on the curb and take a breather.

Hey mom, look at me.

Okay, this is Joey Blumble, reporting. What? You gotta speak up into that thing if you want me to hear you. There you go.

Okay, so the little guy in my ear is telling me that President Puppit has indeed defeated the giant. We don't have more information yet so we don't know exactly how he did it.

You know, I'm gonna ad lib a bit here. I'll tell you, man, this is the stuff of legends what this president has done. If this guy's face isn't on Mount Rushman in a couple of years, I mean, jeez, come on. Right? This is a big f***ing deal.

What? The F word? You can edit that out later, right?

*** END TRANSCRIPT ***

***

Although the House and Senate wings of the Capitol remained mostly undamaged, a massive pile of rubble sat where the Rotunda once stood. A group of police officers kept a growing crowd of onlookers behind yellow caution tape, away from the building.

Brightman stepped behind the mob of spectators. His eyes settled on the Statue of Freedom, the twenty-foot bronze statue that, until moments ago, had graced the top of the Rotunda. Now, it lay on its side, on top of the massive pile of debris.

A young woman approached and stood next to Brightman. "Can you believe--" She stopped midsentence when she realized who she was talking to, then left and joined a small crowd a few feet away. A moment later, others from the group shot a nasty glare to the senator.

Brightman lowered his head and walked toward the side of the building where there were fewer people. As he walked, the clatter of racing footsteps sounded from behind. They slowed when a panting man caught up to him. "Senator Brightman?" the man said.

Brightman stopped and turned square to the stranger. His eyes were immediately drawn to a blue stain on the man's light-colored pants, around the groin.

The man gave an embarrassed chuckle. "Cold-pack ice. Someone kicked me in the ... nevermind." He reached into his pants, pulled the pack out, and tossed it to the side. "My name is Dr. Albert Gress and I have developed potions that alter human DNA. I believe the man that got hold of my potions is the giant destroying the city."

"Why would you invent a potion that makes a man

fifty-feet tall?"

"I didn't plan that," Gress said. "My work is good. My tests were thorough." He began to pace as he spoke. "But something went terribly wrong."

"Why did you come to me?"

"The giant is a colleague of yours. Senator Troller."

"Troller? How did he get the potions?"

"I was lobbying him," Gress said, still pacing. "I needed help loosening some regulations so I could continue my work. I knew I needed someone of questionable character, but when I approached him, he stole my samples." He stopped pacing and stared at Brightman. "There is no way a human can grow to that size without highly complex changes to their DNA. I'm certain it's him."

"You said something went wrong. What were you trying to do?"

"Change people for the better. My potions enhance human DNA. They can turn an ugly man handsome, a short man tall, or a weak man muscular." He closed his eyes. "I didn't know the unintended consequences could be so disastrous."

"Is there a cure? A remedy?"

Gress stopped pacing and snapped his head to attention. His eyes burned through Brightman. "I have spent my life working to progress the human condition. Not to keep it stagnant. And certainly not to revert it."

"Let this get in the wrong hands and it will progress us into oblivion." He looked curiously at Gress. "I still don't know why you came to me?"

"I know how the game is played. I couldn't go to someone of the same political persuasion as Troller or the wagons would begin to circle immediately. You are the most anti-Troller man in Washington."

In spite of the seriousness of the situation, Brightman let a small grin slide onto his face. It was the nicest thing anyone had said to him in a long time. "But it seems your guys already have the situation under control. I saw them take Troller away."

"My guys? I work alone."

Brightman thought back to the helicopters that lured the giant away. He remembered what the men had said: the boss wants to see you. Who is Troller's boss? The president? The Senate Majority Leader? An uneasy feeling settled into the pit of his stomach as he realized the answer to the question. Ultimately, Troller and every other Democrat answered to Joros.

"Where is your work?" he said, turning to Gress. "Your research. We need to get it immediately."

***

The hum of the helicopter crescendoed as it descended onto the landing pad in the courtyard of Joros's mansion.

Inside the mansion, Joros watched through twenty-foot-tall palladium windows. His heart fluttered. A giddy smile overcame him, fed by the anticipation of the power he would soon have.

The ground rocked as the giant approached. He stopped and surveyed the area. Surrounded by woods on three sides, and with a waterfront view, the remote thirty-acre property on the outskirts of Maryland even dwarfed the giant.

He lumbered toward the back of the courtyard where a white vinyl sheet, as tall as the giant himself and equally as wide, hung from the trees. He roared and the thunder from his mouth rattled the trees. Birds scattered. Leaves flew from the branches and danced in the wind. The massive piece of hanging vinyl snapped and rippled in the air.

Joros entered the courtyard. He tilted his head almost directly up and spoke loud. "Welcome, Senator."

Troller grunted, then roared a softer, more amiable roar.

"Sit, please, so we can talk," Joros said.

Troller lowered his body, resting first on his hands and knees, and then working himself to a sitting position to lean his torso against the trunk of a massive oak tree. His legs extended into the center of the courtyard, his head nearly as high as the three-story mansion.

"Just a few minutes ago, my men gave me these." Joros held up a handful of small empty glass vials. "They took the liberty of looking around your apartment. What was left of it, anyway. Is this what you used to become so big and beautiful?"

Troller leaned forward, bringing his face closer to Joros. He fixed his eyes on the glass vials and roared again.

The massive gale slammed Joros. He stepped back, bracing himself against the headwind until it settled. "Why don't you tell me what happened."

"Gress," Troller snarled. "Dr. Gress."

"Dr. Gress? Very interesting." Joros held up the vials again. "Did he give you these?"

Troller nodded. "To make me handsome."

"I see," Joros said. "You are quite handsome."

"No. Was handsome. Then ... don't know."

"Something went wrong, but you can't remember?" Troller nodded.

"Try. Relax. Close your eyes. Think about what happened."

Troller clenched his eyes tight, and his fists tighter. His body trembled as he tried to remember.

"Don't hurt yourself," Joros said. "Are you angry with him? Would you like me to bring Dr. Gress to you?"

Troller struggled to his feet and threw his head back. The loudest of his roars exploded, echoing in the distance.

"I can bring him to you," Joros said. "If you are patient."

Troller swung his arm through the air. It struck the massive oak with a sharp crack, splitting the trunk and sending the top half of the tree falling over. It hit the ground with a thud, and the giant lifted it and tossed it into the woods beyond the courtyard. "Gress," he yelled. With mighty stomps, he headed out of the courtyard.

"Stop." Joros's calm, commanding voice was soft, but it cut through the air.

The giant stopped.

"Down," Joros said, gently patting the air in front of him.

As if attached to Joros's hands by invisible strings, the Democrat eased himself back into a sitting position and leaned against the broken oak tree.

When he was finally seated, Joros stopped his gesturing. He pulled a remote control from his pocket, pointed it at the projector positioned on top of a brick wall opposite the vinyl sheet, and clicked.

A flickering light caught Troller's attention. He twisted to see the display, and an X-rated film lulled the giant into a stupor. He stood for a moment with his mouth open. A stream of drool ran down his chin before dropping to the ground with a splash.

Joros called for his men. "Find Dr. Gress."

CHAPTER 7

The metal safe, two feet wide by two feet tall, sat securely embedded in the concrete wall at the rear of the lab. Gress punched in the password on the control panel and a faint, electric whirring kicked in. The lock disengaged with a click. He swung the door open and removed a thick, over-stuffed loose-leaf binder, placing it on the table in the center of the lab. "That's thirty years of work."

Brightman opened the binder and flipped through it. The pages were packed with mathematical formulas, chemical composition charts, and diagrams. The details made little sense to him, but the enormity of the work was clear.

"Is this everything? What about the potions?"

Gress grabbed a new cold-pack from a small freezer and slid it into the front of his pants, adjusting it into position before answering. "I don't have any more completed ones. Just source ingredients. Follow me."

He led Brightman to a vault at the back of the room. A four-foot-wide stainless-steel door reached from the floor to the ceiling. He pressed down on the handle, opening the six-inch-thick metal slab. A cloud of frozen mist spilled out as he stepped into the freezer.

Brightman followed. The icy air burned his nose as he

breathed in, and thick frost came from his mouth when he exhaled.

Metal shelves, containing racks with thousands of small glass vials, lined the three walls. A thermometer hung from a shelf on the right, displaying the temperature: -30 degrees Fahrenheit.

Brightman took a vial out of one of the racks. He held it up, inspecting it, amazed at how ordinary the tiny sample of clear fluid looked.

"Purified human DNA," Gress said. "You hold in your hand a concentration of the most desirable attributes from some of the most genetically gifted specimens of the human race."

Brightman replaced the vial and took another. He read the handwritten label: male-height-99.99%. He returned it and pulled another: female-eyes-blue-99.98%. "I don't understand. How did you get this?"

"From the specimens themselves, usually. It only takes a small tissue sample. Once you have that, if you understand the genetic map, you can extract the most desirable sequences."

Brightman stepped deeper into the freezer and opened a metal case that sat on the back shelf.

"My gems," Gress said.

Brightman pulled a vial from the case and read the label: Presley. He looked at Gress in amazement. "You don't mean-"

"Yes."

Brightman took another vial: Thorpe. And another: Valentino. "This isn't possible. These people have been dead for years."

"It's very possible. The DNA can come from descendants as well, passed down from one generation to the next. Some attributes may be dormant but, often, they still exist. It then becomes a simple matter of identification, extraction, and purification."

"So, if I drink this, I would turn into a good-looking, hip-grinding, stud?"

Gress chuckled. "Unfortunately, it isn't that simple. These are unrefined samples. They don't possess the carrier agent required to infiltrate and bind with the DNA proteins."

"In English?"

"They might have some effect, but there is no way to know what that effect would be. The range of possibilities is enormous. Any results would certainly be short-lived, and potentially dangerous."

A loud pounding from the other end of the lab echoed, interrupting the men. Gress rushed out of the freezer as Brightman put the vials back in the case and then followed the doctor to the front of the room.

With a crash, the door flew off its hinges. Two men, holding pistols at arm's length, entered the lab. One of the thugs stepped to the table in the center of the room. "What do we have here?" he said, looking at Gress's loose-leaf binder. He approached the doctor. "Are you Gress?"

"Y-y-yes?"

"Over there," the gunman said, motioning with his firearm for the doctor to join the other thug near the door.

Gress, hesitated, looking at Brightman.

"Now," the thug yelled.

Gress obeyed.

The intruder stepped to Brightman and lifted his pistol to the senator's face.

Fear shot through Brightman's body as the cold metal barrel rested on the bridge of his nose.

The thug lifted his eyes, looking over Brightman's shoulder to the back of the room. "Turn around."

Slowly, Brightman turned.

"Walk. Back there."

The gun jammed into Brightman's upper back as he walked toward the freezer. At thirty below, he wouldn't survive long. He had a choice to make, and not much time to make it. He could walk there meekly and meet a slow cold death, or he could fight.

It was an easy choice.

He concentrated on his deliberate footsteps. Left. Right. Left. When his right foot planted again, he pivoted, spun, and pushed off it, lunging at the gunman.

A shot rang out.

Pain burned through his left shoulder. The force of the piercing bullet threw him off balance but in an instant he regained his footing and lunged again.

The gunman raised his leg and kicked, landing his foot square in Brightman's stomach.

Brightman lost his breath. He reeled backwards, stumbling, and fell to the frozen freezer floor. He lifted his head as the door slammed shut, suffocating every trace of sound and light.

****

Dr. Gress ran his fingers along the intricate carvings on the chair moldings. He marveled at the crystal chandelier above and the natural beauty of the marble floor below. As a man whose life was a quest for physical perfection, the lavish interior of Joros's mansion left him breathless. He forgot, for a brief moment, that he had arrived at this glorious place by gunpoint. The reminder came, however, when he turned to find his two captors still standing behind him.

"The brilliant doctor Gress," boomed a voice from across the room. The man who spoke approached with his hand outstretched. "Scourge Joros," he said, taking Gress's hand and shaking it in both of his own. "It is a pleasure and an honor."

Gress hesitated, surprised by Joros's friendly demeanor. "Uh, thank you." He turned again to check on the pair of menacing men behind him.

"Don't mind them," Joros said. "Come." He motioned for Gress to follow as he walked out the French doors that led to another large room--a den with a massive stone mantel and fireplace on the near wall. On the opposite wall, scarlet velvet curtains hung from the twenty-foot-high vaulted ceiling.

Gress followed, scanning the room, still stunned by its exquisiteness.

"There are some who say we cannot attain perfection," Joros said. "What do you think?"

"Something tells me you already know what I think."

"That is correct. So we will move beyond the small talk."

They reached a sitting area in the middle of the room. Two high-backed wing chairs, separated by a coffee table, rested on a large pristine white rug. Joros stepped out of his shoes, sat, and gestured for Gress to take the chair facing him.

Gress leaned in toward the chair, checking the kaleidoscope of colors in the cocobolo's irregular grain as he ran his palm along it. He glanced at Joros, who was nodding approvingly at the doctor's enjoyment of the fine piece of furniture.

Gress removed his shoes and sat, then reached down to inspect the white rug. The soft fur flowed through his fingertips.

"Many years ago I was in South America. I came across a most amazing sight--two incredibly rare albino gorillas. As it turned out, they were the only two known to exist in the world. So, I brought them here and had them turned into this rug. I wanted to make sure their beauty was not wasted."

Gress sat upright and leaned back in the chair. "But you killed them."

Joros Scoffed. "Had I not brought them here, they would have simply died in the jungle, never to be appreciated by anyone. I appreciate perfection and I know that you appreciate perfection as well. Your work proves that."

"I do. But what happened with my potions was a mistake. A terrible accident."

"A great many wonderful things have been created by accident. Someday we will add your work to the list."

Gress slumped in his chair, flinching as the pointed end of the cold-pack in his pants jabbed the inside of his thigh. "Troller never should have taken them," he said as he adjusted the ice pack.

"Ah, Troller," Joros said, inspecting a loose thread on the

sleeve of his mauve silk shirt. "I would be remiss if I didn't tell you he is quite unhappy with you."

"I'm sure he is," Gress said. "But all of this could have been avoided."

Joros unfastened his cuff links and dropped them on the table. He rolled up his left sleeve to identify the source of the rogue thread. "I want your work to continue. I am prepared to give you unlimited financial support."

The words lifted Gress's head.

"Unlimited political support as well," Joros said, struggling, but failing, to secure the thread in his fingertips.

Gress sat fully erect. He pondered what this offer could mean for his vision. The finances, the connections, Joros's own appreciation for perfection. He could continue his quest, realize his dream, and attain perfection.

A man approached and laid two drinks on the table.

Joros held his arm up at length. The man inspected it and pulled the loose thread taut. He lowered his head and grabbed it in his teeth, snapping it off with his bite before leaving. Joros picked up one of the glasses and handed it to Gress, then took the second glass for himself. "To perfection," he said, raising his drink to toast.

"Okay," Gress said, clinking his glass with Joros's. "I'll get back to the lab and find out what went wrong."

"Oh, no," Joros said. "You seem to misunderstand. I want the potions created exactly as they are. I want more giants." He stared off to the side in wonder and spoke in a solemn whisper, "An army of them. An army of my

Democrats tearing the landscape to shreds." He smiled, still looking away, mesmerized by his thoughts.

"But the potions aren't stable. People can get hurt. Besides, I don't even know how it happened. I don't know how he became so large."

Joros snapped out of his daydream.

"I have set up a lab for you in the basement. You'll create more potions. And you will find out how they worked on Troller."

"I'm sorry," Gress said. "I can't do that."

"You seem to misunderstand again," Joros said. "I am not asking you. I have your research. If I had a scientist who could interpret it, you would no longer be here."

Chills climbed Gress's neck. His body tensed in fear, and he felt a steady drip of the cold-pack gel stream down his leg. "I did not spend my life devising a way to create giant monsters."

"Monsters? Doctor, you want your work to change the world, and it can. Our methods may differ but, in the end, we are striving for the same goal. We will create a country, a world, where everything is fair. Where everything is just. Where everything is perfect."

"I'm sorry," he said. "But I can't do that. I think I should go." He put his glass on the table and stood. A flood of blue liquid poured from his pants onto the albino gorilla rug.

Joros seethed when he saw the stain and then stared at Gress with fire in his eyes. "Bring him to the basement," he called across the room.

The two thugs hurried over and seized the doctor.

CHAPTER 8

Nutley studied the broken hinges and the door that lay on the ground. He re-read the address printed on the vial's label, comparing it one more time to the number on the wall. A sense of satisfaction filled him. His reporting instincts were spot on. His hunch was correct. Something had gone down here.

Let the rest of the media world, rank amateurs in his opinion, waste their time on some fifty-foot thing that had already disappeared and was now old news. He was on to something hotter--a big time scandal with a big time name--Senator Brightman--attached to it.

He poked his head through the open doorway and peered around the lab before stepping into the room, his video camera leading the way.

Other than the damage from the obvious break-in, the place had a sterile, clinical appearance. Chemistry, biology, and other science reference books sat neatly lined on the white shelves. The stainless-steel counters shined. But on the far wall, a small safe door hung open.

He checked the safe, finding it empty. As he nosed around the room, a smattering of little red dots, contrasting with the white ceramic tile floor, caught his attention. He inspected them more closely, running his finger through one and holding the crimson stain up to the light.

Blood.

His stomach dropped.

He remained still for a moment, giving his nerves time to settle. But they didn't. He zoomed the camera in for a close-up, growing increasingly anxious as he followed the drops of blood to the back of the room. When the trail stopped in front of a vault door, his anxiety mixed with excitement. Whatever happened here was big.

He hesitated, summoning his courage and mentally preparing for what he might find, then opened the steel door.

A cloud of frost engulfed him. When it dissolved, it revealed a man lying face down, dead, in a pool of frozen blood.

"Jackpot," he said, pumping his fist. He had Brightman on murder. All he had to do was prove the senator's involvement. He hesitated for a moment, letting his good fortune sink in.

He inched closer to the body and tried to flip it over with his foot, but the frozen figure stuck to the vault's floor. The thin room gave him little ability to maneuver, so he grabbed the corpse's feet, yanked hard, and pulled it out of the freezer. He rolled it over onto its back and watched through the camera's viewfinder as the ice on the man's face melted, slowly revealing a clear image.

He gasped, jumping back as he recognized Brightman.

Emotions bubbled deep in his gut. He stepped closer to inspect the body. His adrenaline pumped. This story continued to get better and, as the only one who knew about it, he had it to himself. He could tell it any way he wanted.

He stepped back and took some close-up footage of the body before investigating the vault's contents. A metal case on a shelf in the rear caught his attention. He opened it and pulled out a vial, holding it up to the light to examine it.

Suddenly, he realized something. Here he was, alone, with his political enemy's dead body. Could he be implicated in the senator's death?

Instinctively, he dropped the vial into his jacket pocket and shut the case.

He turned off his video camera. In a panic, he found a cloth in a drawer and wiped down everything he had touched, making sure to leave no fingerprints.

He walked around the door that lay on the floor and headed outside. Checking nervously for security cameras on the way to his car, something occurred to him. Brightman's body was still lying in the middle of the lab, not in the freezer where he found it.

He rushed back inside.

He grabbed the shoulders of Brightman's shirt to pull the body backwards into the vault. With his feet slipping on blood, he gave a giant heave, pulling Brightman's torso up and back.

"Orruuuug." A deep bellowing gurgle came from Brightman's mouth.

Nutley screamed as he released his hands from the shirt and dropped the body. The corpse's head rested on the reporter's shoe.

As the corpse used his foot for a pillow, Nutley paused to compose himself. He had heard that dead bodies make sounds, releasing air as they settle, but had never experienced it himself. He grabbed the shirt again. He tugged hard and stepped back.

"Orrtuuug."

Nutley screamed again and, again, dropped the senator.

Brightman groaned, then coughed. He wasn't dead.

Nutley's heart jumped. A rush of relief flowed through him--he couldn't be implicated in any wrongdoing. He rushed to the front door, lifted it, and propped it up against the frame, jamming a chair behind it to keep it in place.

Brightman groaned again. He worked his way to his hands and knees and rested there a moment, shivering. Using the table for leverage, he got to his feet. He put his right hand on his injured shoulder, grimacing as he tried to lift his left arm. He noticed Nutley. "What are you doing here," he said with a weak voice as he shuddered.

"I was going to ask you the same thing. What did you do with Dr. Gress?" He held the camera in front of Brightman's face for the response.

Brightman looked at the camera with contempt. "Get that out of my face." He said, knocking Nutley's arm away. "Gress," he muttered. "Joros has him."

"Joros? Why would Joros want Gress?"

"For his potions." Brightman staggered to the door.

"What are you talking about?" Nutley put the camera back into Brightman's face. "Where are you going?"

Brightman knocked the camera away again and stuck his finger in Nutley's chest. "Stay away from me." He knocked the chair aside, letting the door fall back on the floor, then went outside, got in his car, and drove away.

Nutley, keeping a safe, undetectable distance behind, followed.

***

Brightman tapped the brakes, keeping the car at a steady pace. He hugged the inside of the narrow winding road and took a quick glance to the left. Even in the dark, the depth of the cliff was clear. Ahead, the glow from Joros's mansion peeked through a thicket of autumn leaves.

He shut the headlights and pulled the car off to the side, grabbed a flashlight from the glove compartment, and then tightened the Velcro strap of his ankle holster. The estate stood about three hundred yards away, but it was safer to finish the trip on foot. There was no reason to risk being seen.

The road tilted into an incline. Thick brush, brought to life by the chattering of crickets, lined each side. He leaned forward as he climbed, following the beam from his flashlight that shined on the ground. His heart pumped hard, delivering a steady throbbing to his wounded left shoulder. The anticipation of not knowing what he would find, or what he would do when he got to Joros's, sparked memories of his combat days, a time when adrenaline and quick thinking ruled the day.

When he reached a high point in the road, his destination became clearly visible. Lights from within the magnificent house glowed with majestic brilliance. Despite its distance, the elements of the dwelling were impressive. Two massive Greek columns stood guard of an oversized double door. Ivy clung to the brick walls, which rose three stories. The entire grounds, completely surrounded by sculpted hedges, sat protected behind a formidable wrought-iron gate. It seemed impenetrable. But, somehow, he had to get in.

As he neared Joros's property, voices from around the next bench stopped him in his tracks. He took cover behind an oak tree and spied on two people who stood a few yards away in front of the opening to the iron gate.

"You ready yet, Blumble?"

"Give me a second, Cratt. These damn things never fit."

Cratt pressed the intercom button on the side of the gate. "Here for Mr. Joros."

With a soft, electric whirring, the gate swung open. Cratt and Blumble entered and headed toward the mansion as the gate closed behind them.

Brightman waited, watching, until they disappeared from view. He shielded the front of the flashlight with his hand, letting just a few rays of light slip between his fingers, and approached the area the men had vacated.

It was a large clearing being used as a parking lot. The vehicles, parked in fairly straight rows of four or five, shared a number of defining characteristics. They were all SUVs, they were all foreign made, and they all had a windshield sticker to allow parking at the U.S. Capitol. It was clear that every car in the lot belonged to a senator. Brightman's gut told him they were all Democrats.

Going down the rows, he gently tried the handle on each one until he came to an unlocked door. Inside, on the seat, he found what he was looking for--a five-by-five card, an invitation, that read "Joros's Annual Birthday Bash--Costumes Required." He dropped the invitation and quietly closed the car door.

There was only one place he could find a costume at this time of night.

***

A new fluorescent "Carson's Uniforms & Costumes" sign hung from the door. The original plastic "Open 24 Hours Through Halloween" sign hung below it.

Brightman peered through the gaping hole in the front of the store. Shards of glass, chunks of plaster, and other debris had been swept into large piles and sat scattered around the floor. Shelving units, mixed with a multitude of costumes and masks, lay in heaps near the back.

He stepped inside, navigated through the mess, and knelt in front of a pile of costumes near the back of the store. He rummaged through the disguises and picked out a pirate sword and eye patch.

The old man he had met earlier, the owner of the business, shuffled forward. "Can I help you?" He took his glasses from his shirt pocket, placed them on his nose, and focused his eyes. "You--you--you," he said, pointing with a shaking finger. "What are you doing here?"

Brightman stood, dropping the patch and sword. "I need a costume."

A door at the back of the room swung open and the old man's son came through. "Surveillance cameras are all set, Pop. Now we'll see who those looters are." He laid his eyes on Brightman. With long, heavy strides he approached the senator. "It's because of you our store looks like this, squealer."

As a sign he wasn't there for trouble, Brightman took a step back. "I'm just looking for a costume."

The large man stepped forward. "We don't have anything."

The man's eyes raged and Brightman retreated again,

until his back hit the wall. He craned his neck slightly to the side and nodded to a pile of costumes in the corner. "Maybe there's something over there."

The man stepped forward again, coming nose to nose with Brightman. "Not for you."

As hot breath fell on his face, Brightman kept his mind focused on getting into Joros's. He knew Joros and Troller, teamed up, would cause more destruction than either could alone. But the man standing in front of him didn't have the slightest idea what was going on. "I need to get a costume or that giant is coming back. And next time he might wipe this place out for good."

The man glared at Brightman. "You threatening me, squealer?"

"No. I didn't mean it that way," Brightman said. "Listen, if I don't get a costume--"

Click.

The old man, hands shaking, aimed a .22 gauge shotgun at Brightman. "I think it's time you leave."

"You don't know what you're doing."

"I know I'm going to shoot you dead if you aren't out of my store in ten seconds."

"You don't understand."

"One."

Brightman stared hard at the man. "Just sell me a costume, and you'll never see me again."

"Two."

Reasoning with this man was clearly not an option. Brightman slipped cautiously away from the wall, past the gun, and approached the exit. He stopped and again considered reasoning with the men.

"Three."

He needed another plan.

He stepped out through the massive hole in the front of the building and into the alcove of a neighboring store. Its facade hung down, smashed the same as Carson's. Looking down the road and across the street, the destruction was everywhere. Knowing how much worse it could get, he gritted his teeth, reached down to his ankle, and unholstered his pistol. He marched back into the store, gun arm extended.

The old man saw him and scampered to reach the shotgun on the counter.

"Freeze," Brightman shouted.

The man stopped in his tracks, and his son moved to stand beside him.

"Over there," Brightman said, using his weapon to point to the corner. He grabbed the shotgun and slid it across the floor in the opposite direction. Scanning the room, he noticed a stack of boxes under the counter.

Keeping his eyes on the men, he slid one box out and slammed the top with the butt of his gun, breaking the tape. He dug his hand in and pulled out the first thing he got hold of--a princess tiara. "Do you guys have anything for grown-ups?"

He pulled out another box, broke the top, and opened the lid. With a deep sigh, he marveled at the absurdity of the masks that filled the box. He grabbed two and held them up--perfect likenesses of himself with a red three-ringed bull's-eye on the forehead. "I guess these will do."

With his gun still pointed at the men, he pulled a

handful of bills from his pocket and tossed the money on the counter. As he walked backwards to the opening, still aiming his gun at the store owners, a glare from above the rear door caught his eye.

He stopped, staring into the lens of a surveillance camera.

***

Brightman stepped past the gate and onto the brick walkway. The path, lined with intricately sculpted hedges, flowing water fountains, and raised gardens, meandered and curved for a quarter mile before meeting the mansion's massive double doors. Two men in black suits and white gloves stood on the sides, stoic as the Queen's Guards. They moved only to open the door for the guest to enter.

The senator adjusted his Brightman-with-a-bull's-eye-on-its-forehead mask and stepped past the guards into the foyer. Behind enemy lines.

"Love the mask," someone said, coming up next to him and putting an arm around his shoulder.

The senator turned to find President Puppit standing next to him. "I'd like to draw a real bull's-eye on that guy's head," the president said with a laugh.

"Uh, yeah, me too," Brightman said. "Hey, no costume for you?"

"Nah. It's not often I get a chance to be myself." He sighed deep and rubbed Brightman's shoulder with a firm grasp. "You know, when Joros picked me, I never dreamed it would work out as well as it has. And from what I hear, we're in for more good news tonight."

"Good news?"

"Probably just confirming we have my next four years in the bag. Maybe even another four after that." He held up two sets of crossed fingers as he walked off.

Brightman scanned the room and spied a congregation of three Democrats. Their costumes--Karl Marx, F.D.R., and a Red Army general--were not unique. They recurred often, along with some Maos, Castros and no less than half a dozen Brightman-with-a-bull's-eye-on-the-foreheads.

He nonchalantly slipped into the group. "How about that giant," he said when there was a lull in the conversation. "Any more news on that?"

"Nope," F.D.R said. "But they say Brightman's behind it. Can't say I'm surprised. It'll be nice when that loser is gone."

The other men agreed, then returned to their storytelling.

Brightman stepped away and scanned the perimeter of the room. At the far end was a hallway, lined with doors. Navigating through the small cliques of party goers, he entered the corridor. After making sure that no one was paying attention to him, he carefully tried the first door.

The moment the handle turned, proving the door was not locked, he knew Gress wasn't inside. Wherever the doctor was, the room would be secure and secluded--maybe upstairs, maybe the basement. Still, one by one, he checked every door, ruling each one out.

Disappointed, he hung his head. His eyes landed on a small blue drop on the floor. He knelt and ran his finger through the liquid. It was slimy. Cold-pack gel.

He followed the drops around the corner, finding one lone door set into an alcove. It was locked. He jammed his good shoulder up against it, braced his feet against the wall, and tried to force it open. It didn't budge. He pulled his pistol from his ankle holster and slammed the door handle with the butt of the gun.

The handle fell to the ground with a clink. He slid it into the corner with his foot and opened the door. After closing it behind him, he moved slowly down the basement steps. At the bottom, in the corner, sat Gress, gagged and tied to a chair.

Brightman worked the gag away from the doctor's mouth and then untied his feet and hands. "Where is your work?"

"In here." Gress opened a cabinet on the side of the room. Inside was the binder of his research papers and six small vials. "There are potions too. He had me make more. He's going to create an entire army of giants."

Brightman pulled the extra mask from inside his jacket and handed it to Gress to put on. He nudged Gress out of the way and grabbed the potions. He didn't trust anyone with them, not even the man who created them.

One by one, he gently placed the glass vials in his shirt pocket. He snapped open the binder and quickly leafed through the pages. Knowing how important the information was to the nation's security, he pulled them out. "Take these," he said, shoving them at Gress.

The doctor jammed the papers into his socks, his underwear, and under his shirt, smoothing them out so no bulges could be seen.

Brightman headed back up the stairs as Gress followed. At the top, he cracked open the door and peeked out. The coast was clear. He turned back to Gress. "We don't have much time. Once they realize you're gone, the place will be on lockdown."

The two men stepped into the hallway and entered the ballroom.

"Follow me," Brightman said, heading for the front door.

As they approached, the guard held his hand up at arm's length. "No one leaves until Mr. Joros speaks."

"Attention, everyone." The voice boomed over a microphone. Joros, in a black tuxedo and top hat, stood behind a podium at the far end of the room. "Come," he said, motioning for Brightman and Gress. "You must not leave now."

"Let's not look suspicious," Brightman whispered to Gress. They joined the crowd in the back of the room. "But be ready. The minute this is over, we're out of here."

CHAPTER 9

Joros spoke into the microphone, interrupting the chatter and bustling of the crowd. "As you are all aware, there was quite a bit of commotion in the city this morning. I am happy to tell you our friends in the media have been doing their job well. Make no mistake that public suspicions will be properly directed at the Republicans."

A soft applause arose and Joros waited before continuing. "But that is not the exciting part. What you do not know is that the giant we saw this morning is actually one of us--our very own Senator Troller."

A smattering of cheers filled the room.

"And," Joros said, quieting everyone with his hands. "I have found the man responsible for Troller's impressive size."

The applause returned, this time louder.

"Each year, we meet to discuss important issues. Most notably, the best way to move this country forward. It seems we now have a strategy that cannot be matched. After the election, after we have officially retained control of the government, I will unleash an army of giants that will help us transform this country faster and more completely than we ever dreamed possible. They will tear down everything that stands in our way."

Applause and cheering filled the room, forcing Joros to

raise his voice to a yell. "And then we will rebuild this country in my vision."

The crowd erupted.

"The vision you all have worked hard to help bring about."

Hoots, hollers, and whistles rang from each corner of the room.

"Now," Joros said, "your president will say a few words."

President Puppit approached the podium as two men wheeled in a teleprompter and positioned it in the front of the podium. "I want to also thank everyone," the president said, reading from the prompter.

After just those few words, a guest in the front of the crowd wobbled and stumbled.

The president giggled. "Looks like someone is a little star-struck."

The guest, with what appeared to be well-groomed, Friedrich Engels facial hair, stumbled again, then dropped to the ground.

"I think we need a little help up here," the president said.

A Stalin impersonator pushed his way forward. "Look out. Out of the way. I'm a doctor. Give him some space." He kneeled over the body and pulled off the visitor's mask. A hush fell over the room.

Brightman bobbed and weaved, trying unsuccessfully, to find an opening in the crowd to peer through.

"This looks like that reporter," Stalin said.

Joros marched over. "Clear away."

The crowd dispersed, revealing Merv Nutley lying on

the ground, clutching his leg.

"How did he get in here?" Joros said. "Take him!"

One of the two guards from the front door left his post and rushed over to seize Nutley, holding him up from under his arms as the reporter's legs flopped freely in the air.

"Let's get out of here," Brightman said to Gress, looking to take advantage of the confusion. They headed toward the front door at half-walk, half-run speed.

"In line, everyone," Joros said. Even without the microphone, his voice carried throughout the room.

The guard that remained at the door stood tall and crossed his arms as Brightman and Gress approached.

Brightman halted. He turned to find all of the guests scurrying to line up, shoulder to shoulder, in the center of the room.

With no choice but to join the line, he squeezed his way in near the middle. Gress wedged in next to him.

Composed of about fifty people, the line stretched from one end of the room to the other. Joros stepped front and center. "I don't know how he got in here," he said, pointing to Nutley in the guard's grip. "But if there is anyone else that doesn't belong, I intend to find them."

Brightman eyed the door. It was about fifty feet away and the large guard still blocked it. "Be ready if we get a chance to run for it," he whispered to Gress.

"Drop them," Joros demanded of everyone that stood before him.

Every guest to the left and right of Brightman and Gress dropped his pants to their ankles.

Brightman leaned back and glanced to his left. Then to his right. On the left cheek of every senator's bottom was a large branding, something Brightman hadn't seen in over two decades--D.U.M.I.

Before he could even process what this meant, Joros had stepped behind Brightman, grabbed his pants by the pockets, and yanked them down to the floor.

The crowd gasped at the unmarked rear.

Joros pantsed Gress.

The crowd gasped again.

Joros pulled off Brightman's mask. He sneered, then ripped off the doctor's mask. "Take them to the back. Along with that reporter. I'll deal with them later."

The guard dragged Nutley by the shirt with one hand and approached Brightman.

Without hesitating Brightman lunged at the thug, pushing him back and sending him stumbling to the floor. "Come on," he called to Gress. He pulled up his pants and raced to the front of the room. As he ran, he locked his sights on the guard that stood at the front door. He was a large man, but Brightman would have momentum.

The guard, however, didn't stay in place. He ran toward Brightman at full speed.

Brightman disregarded his bullet wound and lowered his shoulder.

The men collided with a bone-cracking crunch.

Glass shattered. The vials.

The guard wrapped his arms around Brightman as he continued barreling forward like a freight train, sending the senator flying backwards like a tackling dummy.

Brightman turned to see the wall flying closer as he glided back. He swiped at the guard's legs with his feet, tripping him, and the guard stumbled forward, falling on the senator. The two men slid across the floor until they crashed against the base of the wall.

Brightman, buried under his opponent, pounded the man's side with his fist and pushed his way out from underneath. He scanned the room, orienting himself and looking for a way out.

In the center of the room, a small puddle from the liquid of the broken vials bubbled, releasing a thin line of black smoke. The bubbling quickly intensified--and the black smoke thickened.

As the guard staggered to his feet and rushed Brightman, the senator grabbed the man--one hand on his waist and the other on his arm. With one massive heave, he threw the guard to the side, sending him stumbling, headfirst into the curtain, pulling it from its hangers at the ceiling. Wrapped and covered in the red velvet drape, he fell forward, crashing through the palladium window into the courtyard. The shattering echoed as twenty feet of glass fell to the ground. When it stopped, silence hung over the room. Everyone in attendance stood, unmoving, stunned at what they saw through the window opening.

In the courtyard, sitting up against a tree, was Troller. The giant leaned his massive head forward and peered into the room. "Gress," he yelled when he spotted the doctor.

The partiers panicked, ran in circles, and looked for cover.

With the front door unguarded, Brightman grabbed Gress. "Hurry," he said, pulling on the doctor's arm.

But the doctor didn't move.

Brightman tugged harder. "Come on." He looked down

to find Nutley lying on the ground, clinging to Gress's leg.

"Don't leave me here," Nutley cried.

Troller stepped forward, breaking through the wall and ripping into the ceiling. The back section of the mansion's roof crumbled. In the center of the room, thick black smoke rose up from where the potion had spilled. It hung in the air, blanketing the room.

"That's it," Gress said. "That's how it happened. Don't breathe this."

As the smoke thickened, Brightman pulled Nutley from Gress's leg. He flung the crippled man over his shoulder and raced through the front door.

***

Moans and groans spewed from the moonlit mansion, hanging in the air as thick and heavy as the black smoke that oozed out of the windows.

Troller toppled the side wall as he lumbered into the courtyard.

Nutley, draped over Brightman's shoulder and videoing the scene, bounced up and down as the senator raced across the grounds.

A faint crackling electrified the air. It grew louder and more intense, like popcorn over a fire. When it stopped, an eerie silence loomed, and a creaking overpowered the silence.

A giant head hatched through the rooftop.

The giant body that the head belonged to stood fully erect and stepped forward, joining Troller.

Another giant poked through the roof. Then another.

The mansion's front wall crumbled. In a matter of moments, the house was reduced to a pile of rubble beneath the feet of an army of fifty-foot Democrats.

Joros stood off to the side, dwarfed by his Democrat comrades, giddy and yelling with glee, pointing into the distance. "Go. Transform this country. Transform it." He fell to his knees and howled with pleasure as the Democrats scattered, obeying his command.

Nutley craned his neck and looked down at the man that carried him to safety. His stomach sank. Brightman wasn't the culprit. Had he been wrong about the senator all along? Was Brightman actually a decent man? No. These were extraordinary circumstances and those ridiculous ideas needed to be pushed out of his mind, pushed to the side and completely ignored. Whether Brightman was involved in this or not wasn't the issue. If he was to get his show back, the only thing that mattered was following this story through. And what a story it had become.

"Troller," Joros called in the distance. "Get Brightman. Get Gress. Get Nutley."

Brightman flung open the gate and raced across the parking lot to a clearing in the woods, then dumped Nutley on the ground at the top of a small hill.

Nutley, protecting his video camera, hit the ground with a thud. Brightman, hunched over and gasping for breath, pushed Nutley with his foot, sending him rolling down the hill. Twigs and rocks jabbed him as he tumbled down. When he stopped, he looked up to see Brightman grab Gress's arm and pull the doctor down the slope.

The three men hid among the bushes.

Nutley focused his camera for the once-in-a-lifetime footage but Brightman swatted it down. "You want to get us killed? No lights. No sound."

Troller stepped into the parking lot. One by one the giant picked up an SUV, brought it to his face, and peered inside. When he didn't find the men he was looking for, he tossed it over the trees into the wilderness. After disposing of all the vehicles, he roared and headed down the road.

When he was out of sight, the three men climbed back up to the road.

"Oh, God," Gress cried as he paced. "What have I done? What have I done?"

"Take it easy," Brightman said, putting his hand on the doctor's shoulder.

Gress leapt back. His head darted left, then right.

"Easy, Doc. It's just me," Brightman said.

Gress stared at Brightman as if he didn't know him, then looked around like he didn't know where he was.

"He's losing it," Nutley said.

"Doc," Brightman said. "Relax. Come on. Let's go."

"Go? To where? There is nowhere we can go and nothing we can do. We can't stop them."

"We're not going to sit out here and do nothing," Brightman said.

"There is only destruction and death that way," Gress said, pointing in the direction Troller had gone. "We have to go this way." He pointed in the opposite direction.

Brightman stuck his finger in the doctor's face. "You created them. You're going to help stop them."

"No," Gress said, walking backwards. "I'm staying

away from those monsters." He turned and ran, disappearing into the woods.

"What do we do now?" Nutley said, fiddling with his camera and making sure it was still in working order.

Brightman ignored the question and started down the winding dirt road.

***

*** BREAKING NEWS ***

*** WILL WILLIAMS REPORTING ***

*** BEGIN OFFICIAL TRANSCRIPT ***

WILL WILLIAMS: Hello everyone, I'm Will Williams.

In yet another dramatic turn of events, the giant Republican monster that was on the loose yesterday morning is on the rampage again. And this time, there are dozens more just like him. You heard right--dozens of Republican monsters on the loose and on the way to destroying every corner of the country.

It seems a well-known Republican senator has been behind this from the very beginning. You might recognize him from this surveillance video taken just a few hours ago as he robbed a local business at gunpoint.

(START VIDEOTAPE)

BRIGHTMAN: Freeze!

Over there.

Do you guys have anything for grown-ups?

I guess these will do.

(END VIDEOTAPE)

WILL WILLIAMS: For those of you that don't know him, that is the traitorous senator, Bart Brightman, holding two helpless citizens at gunpoint. But Senator Brightman is not working alone. He is just the ringleader of this operation.

The brains behind it all? Geneticist Dr. Albert Gress. A scientist who apparently has created some kind of potion to turn Republicans into giants. He is a private man, there isn't much detail on him yet, although we are working feverishly behind the scenes to find out all of the information we can.

And the final accomplice? Disgraced talk show host, Merv Nutley. Now, we've done a little digging through his medical records--can I say we did that?

UNIDENTIFIED MAN, OFF CAMERA: No. You really shouldn't be saying that. Not to millions of people.

WILL WILLIAMS: Oh, okay, well, um, it has somehow come to our attention that Nutley was recently referred to a psychologist. The extent of his mental problems are not yet clear.

But there you have it. A traitor, an evil scientist, and a loon: Brightman, Gress, and

Nutley.

If you see any of these men, they are to be considered armed and dangerous. Do not approach them. And do not, under any circumstances, attempt to interfere with the giants. You are asked to remain inside. A declaration of national emergency is expected shortly.

Now, we always want to give as much insight as possible and we have been trying to get one of our trusted guests, but our Democratic senators are nowhere to be found. Apparently, they have already gotten a jump and are planning and plotting ways to stop these giant beasts. So, instead, we have Republican Senator Barney Jaxon joining us in the studio.

Barney, I'm glad to see you haven't turned into a giant like the other Republicans.

BARNEY JAXON, GEORGIA SENATOR: Actually, I'm not so sure that--

WILL WILLIAMS: What do you make of Brightman holding up two citizens at gunpoint?

BARNEY JAXON: Well, I don't think we can jump--

WILL WILLIAMS: Oh, come on. He acted stupidly. Admit it.

BARNEY JAXON: I understand your position and I fully respect--

WILL WILLIAMS: No you don't. Since when do Republicans respect anything?

BARNEY JAXON: Well, I think--

WILL WILLIAMS: No you don't. Since when do Republicans think?

BARNEY JAXON: Ok, look. I think if we want to discuss the problem at hand, then there are probably many things we can agree on. For example, as far as declaring a national emergency, I agree 100 percent and I think President Puppit--

WILL WILLIAMS: I don't think I like that tone.

BARNEY JAXON: What tone? I just said I agree 100 percent with President Puppit and--

WILL WILLIAMS: Ohhhhhh. There it is again.

BARNEY JAXON: There what is again?

WILL WILLIAMS: The way you say his name.

BARNEY JAXON: How am I saying his name?

WILL WILLIAMS: Why do you hate our president?

BARNEY JAXON: I'm not sure what you mean. Look, all I'm saying is--wait--what--what are you doing?

WILL WILLIAMS: Nothing.

BARNEY JAXON: You're undressing.

WILL WILLIAMS: No I'm not.

BARNEY JAXON: Your shirt is off.

WILL WILLIAMS: No it's--oh goodness, it's happening again.

BARNEY JAXON: Stop that. Please. I feel a

little uncomfortable right now.

WILL WILLIAMS: Look, why don't we just act professional about this and continue? Can we do that?

BARNEY JAXON: Professional? Okay. I, um, what was I saying? Oh, right. Well, I think President Puppit is--hey, stop that.

WILL WILLIAMS: Stop what?

BARNEY JAXON: Why are you taking your clothes off?

WILL WILLIAMS: I, uh, I really don't know.

BARNEY JAXON: What are you doing now?

Get off the table.

Leave those on.

Please.

(ADULT CONTENT)

(PROGRAM INTERRUPTED)

*** END TRANSCRIPT ***

CHAPTER 10

As Brightman continued along the desolate dirt road, he dialed Colonel Stupp on his cell. Intermittent static and silence broke up the connection. Far from the city and shrouded by the dense fall foliage, his phone could muster only half a bar of power.

"Where are we going?" Nutley asked, shuffling quickly with his limp leg in tow. He worked hard to match Brightman's brisk pace and keep the video camera aimed at the senator.

Brightman turned and scowled, but said nothing, then set his eyes back on the road ahead.

Nutley waited a minute before repeating his question.

Brightman huffed, shook his head, and ignored it again. It wasn't until the question had been asked a half-dozen more times that he decided to answer. "McCleary Air Force Base."

"What for?"

"I have a contact there. Maybe a way to stop these giants. Maybe. If the base hasn't been destroyed." He glared at Nutley. "Turn that damn camera off."

For the next few hours, neither man spoke. Brightman, walking ten paces in front of Nutley, spent the time imagining the destruction he was sure to find when they reached the city. When the sun finally rose above the horizon, peeking through gaps in the trees, the hum of a motor grew out of the silence behind them. Brightman waved his arms to flag down the vehicle. "Any word on the giants?" he said as the driver rolled down the window of his pickup truck. "Have they reached the city?"

"They're all over the East Coast and heading west, destroying everything in their path."

"Any help at all? Feds? Locals?"

"Nothing. I'm going to D.C. There's a group of us going to take one of them down."

"I need to get to McCleary Air Force Base. Can you give me a lift?"

"Hop in. I'm not going that far but maybe you can find another ride when we get to D.C."

Brightman and Nutley climbed into the open trailer next to a pile of rifles and a case of ammunition. A half hour later, the truck pulled up to the National Mall and stopped on a large grass field near Constitution Gardens. A few small packs of civilians, seven or eight per group, armed with everything from rifles to shotguns to crossbows, wandered about the immediate area between the Lincoln and Vietnam Veterans memorials.

The driver popped out of the front seat. "Maybe one of these folks will lend you a car," he said, reaching into the rear of the pickup and grabbing a rifle. "But we can use all the help we can get if you want to stick around."

"I like your thinking, but I'll pass," Brightman said. "It's not going to be easy taking this giant down."

"Oh, it's going down all right." The man cocked his gun and aimed his sight in the distance, high in the air. "Pow," he said, pretending to shoot a giant.

"Senator Brightman?" said a voice from one of the small crowds. A man came forward and offered his hand. "Natanio Halendros. It's good to finally meet you. Although the conditions could have been better."

"I need a car," he said as he shook Halendros's hand. "I have to get to McCleary Air Force Base."

"What for? There's no military to help. We're the last line of defense. The only line of defense."

Brightman scanned the area. These people weren't soldiers. Sure, they might be gung ho about going after the giant now, but that would all change when they actually came face to face with the monster. "You guys won't be able to handle one of these giants, let alone a couple of dozen all across the country. I have a connection at McCleary. There may be just enough military muscle left and I might be able to get my hands on it."

"Come with me," Halendros said. He walked back behind the cars to an area with four folding tables covered with supplies--a makeshift satellite dish, a ham radio, boxes of flares, and first-aid kits. A dozen laptops, powered by a portable, gas-driven generator, sat on another table.

"We're not alone," Halendros said. He flipped up a laptop screen. Video streamed, showing a similar, small group of armed civilians. "This is Denver. They're getting ready." He switched to a different screen with video of another group. "This is Houston. We've got chapters all across the country."

A man hurried to the table and set down another

laptop. "Natanio, we have Philadelphia online."

The laptop's speakers screeched as bouncy, amateur camera work filled the screen with footage of a giant romping through the city. It showed the monstrous Democrat stepping through buildings, sending walls toppling with plumes of dust and debris filling the air. He stopped in front of an old brick building.

"That's Independence Hall," Brightman said.

The giant spread his arms wide, then sent them crashing together, clapping them on the steeple of the historic site. As the structure splintered between the two massive hands, a high-pitched chime sounded. The Liberty Bell flew from the steeple and landed on the ground nearby. The giant picked up the bell. Holding it between his thumb and forefinger, he lifted it above his head and rung his new toy as he lumbered down the road.

Halendros closed the laptop screen.

"Going after these giants is a death sentence," Brightman said.

"What choice do we have? Wait for Canada and Mexico to save us? You might have something up your sleeve at McCleary, but if not, then what?"

Brightman looked again at the faces around him. It was a small, diverse group--young and old, men and women, black and white--typical grassroots, a perfect cross section of America. But they weren't soldiers, and they had no business acting like they were. "These people aren't prepared for this."

"They will fight for their country. They will die for their country if they have to."

Brightman let the words sink in. They were heavy words, and they reminded him of the men he commanded decades ago. The men he was responsible for. The men he ultimately betrayed. It didn't matter how many times he told himself it wasn't his fault, and it didn't matter that it really wasn't his fault. He scanned the crowd again. No, they weren't ready, and if they wanted to fight, he wasn't about to get involved. "It's your choice," Brightman said. "Can you get me a car?"

Halendros tossed his keys to Brightman. "Good luck," he said, patting the senator on the shoulder.

A sharp pain shot down Brightman's arm. He winced and clutched his shoulder.

Halendros pulled Brightman's collar down. "That's a nasty wound. Let's clean it out." He rummaged through the supplies on the table and opened a first-aid kit, laying out a roll of gauze and opening a bottle of hydrogen peroxide. He pulled Brightman's shirt to the side again, then paused.

He lifted the hemp necklace from the senator's neck, cradling the halved silver dollar in his hand.

"It's from my combat days," Brightman said.

Halendros pulled a thin necklace from under his own shirt.

Brightman leaned closer, staring in amazement at the mating piece to his medallion.

***

Nutley found a row of cherry trees alongside a walkway and sat himself, leaning up against one. After making sure no one was near, he turned his camera on and set it to playback mode. As he fast-forwarded and rewound through the footage, scanning the events of the last few days, a surge of excitement ran through him. It was all coming together. He had the story nobody else had. The story that was sure to put him back on top.

But there was still a ton of editing to do in order to get it the way he wanted. He scanned the footage again, making mental notes of where best to cut and splice scenes in order to subvert context and maximize Brightman's implication.

Off to the side, Brightman and Halendros were engaged in what seemed to be intense dialog. Nutley stretched out his arms, making a frame in the air with his fingers and centering the men. Perfect. From a distance, the imagery could easily lead one to the conclusion that they were plotting something sinister.

As he turned his camera to recording mode, the guilt he felt when he was flung over Brightman's shoulder resurfaced. Could he do this story, he wondered, without implicating Brightman? No. Absolutely not. Well, maybe. It might be possible, but without Brightman it lost its scandalous element--and its greatest villain. Once again, he pushed the guilt aside.

He lifted his camera, aimed it at the two men, and zoomed in. With his mouth near the microphone, he narrated in a smooth, clear tone.

"Senator Bart Brightman, with Natanio Halendros and his gang of right-wing extremists, prepare to unleash more havoc and destruction on this country than it has ever seen."

He paused the camera and doubted himself again. Did he really need this scene? He probably had enough footage already. Besides, too much video would just make editing that much more difficult. He shut the camera off. Why complicate things? Brightman wasn't really such a bad guy. It's not like he *needed* to implicate Brightman. With a deep breath, he leaned his head back against the trunk of the cherry tree, relaxing from the rigors of the last two days. His eyes grew heavy and began to close.

He jerked his head forward.

Of course he needed to implicate Brightman! Obviously, he was exhausted and not thinking straight. This was an opportunity to nail Brightman and Halendros at the same time. He turned his camera back on, aimed it at his two unknowing subjects, and zoomed in.

He focused his thoughts, then added more narration. When he ran out of space on the current disc, he switched the camera to playback mode and reviewed his work.

It was perfect. He was that much closer to getting back on top.

***

"I still remember when he cut this in half," Halendros said, joining the two medallions. "He did it with his pocket knife. It took him all day."

Brightman dropped his head and set his eyes on the ground. Feeling responsible for the death of Halendros's father, it was nearly impossible to look the young man in the eye.

"He gave it to me just a few days before he was captured," Halendros said.

Brightman's mind wandered back twenty-five years to the short time he spent in captivity with Halendros's father. "They killed him."

"I know. I snuck into the camp each night but I never found him. I saw you, hanging by your hands, but I never saw him again after that day." He chuckled. "All these years, I had no idea you were the American." He poured the hydrogen peroxide onto Brightman's shoulder.

The disinfectant bubbled and burned, but Brightman didn't flinch. His mind was locked on Halendros and his followers, and the battle they were preparing for. He knew he wouldn't be able to change Halendros's mind about fighting the giant. He also knew that if the rag-tag army was to have any chance at all, it needed help. "I guess your guys can use a quick boot camp before going into battle."

"Yes." Halendros smiled. "Let's introduce you." He finished bandaging Brightman's shoulder and turned to the scattered cliques of troops. "Everyone, gather around."

The groups came forward and blended together as Halendros introduced Brightman.

It had been a long time since Brightman was in the midst of a favorable crowd. The faces were eager, and they looked excited to have authentic military experience on board. He suppressed a smile, basking in the fact that they respected him. He scanned the new unit, making eye contact and nodding to as many as he could.

They were attentive and poised, all of them. Except one.

The young man from Carson's Uniforms & Costumes stepped forward. "They say squealer here's the one that let the giants loose in the first place." He turned to address the crowd. "I bet there's a nice reward for him. I say we collect. Who's with me?"

"I got you, buddy," one man said. He took a drag of his

cigarette, flicked it away, and stepped next to Carson.

Two others came forward and joined.

"When you find this giant, you gonna confess him to death?" Carson said, approaching Brightman and staring down at him. "Tell him all your secrets till he just keels over? Get someone's hands chopped off?"

The lingering anger of the last four years erupted in Brightman. In one swift motion, he grabbed Carson by the throat and knocked the rifle out of his hand. He clutched the big man's windpipe with just less than enough pressure to snap it as he forced him backwards up against the side of a truck. He held him there, pinned against the pickup, and stared into the man's eyes.

It was a few moments before he realized what he had done. His anger cooled, slowly, and turned to shame. He loosened his grip and stepped back.

Carson gasped for air. After catching his breath, he motioned for his three followers to get in the truck. He got behind the wheel, and revved the engine. The tires screeched as he raced away.

**

Brightman stepped off to the side, alone, to collect himself. He was shocked and disgusted at the way he had just acted. But an instant later, he was surprisingly calm. It was as if the explosion within him burned up every available ounce of anger, leaving him completely depleted of the emotion.

He stared out at the people gathered in the field, proud of what they wanted, what they were willing to do, and what they stood for. A simple realization that had been lost on him for years suddenly settled. It didn't matter what any of his detractors said or did. What mattered were the people out there willing to fight--willing to die--for what they believed in.

Out of the corner of his eye, he noticed Nutley sitting up against a tree. It was time to leave the nonsense between the two of them in the past. It was also time to get all hands on deck and prepare to battle the giant Democrats. Nutley may have been a spectator until now, but this rag-tag army would need all the help they could get.

He approached the ex-journalist and hovered above him. He watched along on the camera's LCD as Nutley, unaware someone was standing over him, played through the videos.

With each clip, it became clearer to Brightman what he was looking at. It wasn't a documentary of the events or a behind-the-scenes exposé. It was a hit piece--and he was the target.

Finally, Nutley looked up. He slapped his camera's screen closed. "Um, what's up?"

"Interesting footage."

"Oh, yeah," Nutley said, breaking eye contact. "A couple of good clips, I guess."

"Don't think I don't know what you're doing."

"What? What are you talking about?"

Brightman scoffed, shaking his head. "You think I expect anything that resembles the truth to come out of that camera?"

"Everything I report is the truth," Nutley said. "Believe me, Joros will be running for the hills when I'm done." He tried to make this sound honest and authentic, but he failed miserably.

"Have fun with your story," Brightman said, stepping past Nutley and back toward the field of soon-to-be soldiers. "I don't care any more."

***

Fall in," Brightman yelled.

The troops looked around at each other with puzzled expressions.

"That means everyone over here," Brightman said, pointing to the ground in front of him. "Single file."

After everyone stumbled into a straight line, he studied their faces again. They were nothing like the soldiers he had worked with in the past. They were untrained and clearly less physically adept. He knew there wasn't a minute of combat experience between them. But they stood tall and ready, looking back at their new leader with attention and allegiance. It was a look that soothed him, a look that he hadn't seen from anyone in a long time.

But in the back of his mind, a simple question nagged. Were they ready? He knew they were going to fight with him or without him, so the answer was simple. It was his job to make them ready.

"Anybody can pull a trigger," Brightman said. "But all victories, big and small, need a plan, a strategy. The better our strategy, and the better we learn it and stick to it, the better chance we have of coming out of this in one piece. The most important thing to remember is that we are a team. I've got your back and you've got mine. Take a look at everyone standing with you. You've all got each other's backs. Now, we're going to make this simple. We'll create two flanks."

With his hand, he divided the line into two halves. "Everyone on the left side of the line will be the left flank. Everyone on the right side will be the right flank. When we find the giant, we'll attack him from two sides, the left and the right. Never the front and back. We need to stay out of his direct line of sight as much as possible. The better we can do that, the more we can keep him off guard."

A boy that appeared to have not yet hit his twenties raised his hand.

"Yes?" Brightman said.

"What if we can't keep him off guard?" the boy's voice cracked as he spoke.

"Then we're in trouble," Brightman said.

"I say we're in trouble either way," said someone else from the line. "Let's face it, these things are freaking tremendous."

Fear overran the young boy's face and the troops began to chatter among themselves.

Brightman scanned the lineup from one end to the other. The boy wasn't alone. There was plenty of fear. The realization that many of these people were making--that they didn't know what they were getting themselves into at first, but did now--sobered him. They weren't soldiers. He stepped back, putting some distance between himself and the troops as the banter continued.

"Are we going to get back to training?" said a voice from the line.

Brightman ignored the question and waved Halendros

over. "There is no way this will work," he said softly. "There's no way this group is going to be able to handle that giant. I don't know what I was thinking."

"They want to fight," Halendros said. "You can't stop them."

"Then you have to stop them. Buy some time. I didn't save your life twenty-five years ago to watch you throw it away today."

"You didn't do it to watch me sit around while our country gets destroyed, either."

Brightman looked beyond Halendros. In the distance, a flare lit the sky. Moments later, the dreadful but familiar rumble of a giant's stomping shook the ground.

Continuous honking rang through the air as Carson's truck raced toward them. His three companions stood in the back of the truck, yelling, "Here he comes. Get ready." They fired another flare.

Troller followed, swatting the flare out of the sky.

Brightman took a final look around at the rag-tag army. Ready or not, they were going into battle.

CHAPTER 11

Joros sat at the desk in his White House office, leaning forward on the edge of his padded swivel chair. He pressed the speaker button on the phone and spoke to Shepherd on the other end. "Find all three of them."

"Our investigative department is on it, sir."

Joros clicked the phone off, clenched his fist, and gently pounded the desktop. The idea of Brightman, Nutley, and Gress still roaming free vexed him. They had seen everything, and knew too much. There was no telling what kinds of problems they could cause. They had to go. But first, he had to find them.

A knock on the door interrupted his thoughts.

"Come in."

President Puppit and Press Secretary Gray entered.

"Mr. Joros," Gray said in a panic, "the people are getting impatient. They want to know why we haven't unleashed our Canadian and Mexican allies on the giants. They're starting to think that NAMCA was a mistake."

Joros focused on the president's dark slacks. "That crease," he said with a befuddled look.

Puppit smoothed out his pant leg. "What?"

"It is hardly presidential. It should be crisp and tight. Sharpen it."

"Mr. Joros," Gray said. "The giants?"

Joros fixed an expression of stone on his face, but inside he cringed. Why didn't he corral the Democrats the moment they became giants? He had planned on finding a way to release giants after the election, but when it happened by accident, well, what a wonderfully exciting accident it was. He had immediately envisioned his Democrats running rampant from coast to coast, frolicking on the grounds of the nation's hallowed landmarks. In that moment of weakness, his emotions got the better of him, and he let the giants out too early.

"Stall," he said, leaning back in his chair and resting his feet on the desk. "We only have five more days before the election."

Gray stepped forward and leaned on the desk. "We need to do something now."

Joros stared at Gray's hands at the edge of his desk, then fixed his eyes on the face of the man who just dared to tell him what to do.

"I mean," Gray said, "I think that we should, maybe, do something sooner, sir." He stood upright and shuffled back. "I'm afraid we might even lose votes because of this."

The words hit Joros hard. Losing votes was not acceptable. "Suspend the election."

"Are you sure?" Gray said. "For how long?"

"Indefinitely."

Joros looked to President Puppit. "You'll address the country tomorrow. You'll reassure everyone we have the situation under control but that, for their safety, the elections are postponed. I'll write the speech."

Puppit gingerly cleared his throat. "I was, uh, thinking maybe I could do it on my own this time."

"No," Joros said, shaking his head slowly. "This is too

important."

"I really think I'm ready."

Joros sighed. "What happened the last time I let you speak on your own? That speech at the hospital closing."

"Oh come on. You can't count that."

"What happened?"

"I forgot ..." Puppit's words trailed off into a mumble as his chin dropped to his chest.

"Louder."

"I forgot pneumonia had a silent 'p.'"

"You forgot?"

Puppit huffed. "Fine. I didn't know. But I never saw the word before. How was I supposed to know. You can't count that. It's not fair."

"Mm-hmm," Joros said. "And what happened that time you and the first lady spoke from the White House garden? You were talking about nutrition, explaining to the kids how to make a fruit smoothie."

Puppit dropped his eyes to the floor.

"Well?" Joros said.

"I forgot ..." his words trailed off into a mumble again.

"Louder."

"I forgot--I didn't know raspberry had a silent 'p.'" He stamped his foot. "But I know all the 'p' words now," he said, his eyes wide and his voice full of energy. "Pseudonym. Psychiatrist. Even coup and corps."

"Mm-hmm," Joros said. "Finish this sentence: We are running a forty-trillion-dollar national ...?"

"Debit," Puppit shouted with proud excitement. "Debit ... card?"

Gray leaned over and whispered into Puppit's ear.

"Oh," Puppit said, slouching his shoulders. "Debt."

Joros, eyebrows raised, gazed at the president. "Maybe we should use the prompter."

Puppit crossed his arms across his chest. "Fine."

"Good," Joros said. "Gray, set everything up to have it broadcast."

"Yes, sir," Grey said before he and Puppit left the room.

Joros planted his feet back on the ground and leaned forward, forearms on the desk. He tapped his fingers as he thought again about the mistake of letting the giants loose too early. How could he have been so foolish? As he played through the events of the last few days, searching for more loose ends, the phone rang.

He pressed the speaker button. "Yes?"

"We have a lead on Brightman, sir," Shepherd said.

"Where is he?"

"Well, we don't know his location. But we went over his phone records and he tried to make a call just a few hours ago."

"To whom?"

"Colonel Stupp. He's the commanding officer at McCleary."

"I know who he is."

"What are our next steps, sir?"

"You worry about the news," Joros said. "I'll take care of this."

***

The giant approached Constitution Gardens, stomping

on the Federal Reserve Building in his path. The building's side wall toppled, the roof collapsed, and a plume of smoke and dust rose into the air.

He kicked through the Vietnam Memorial. The gabbro rock wall exploded, shattering and sending pieces flying through the air. Mounds of dirt and grass, kicked up along with it, followed. When the giant stopped, he stood twenty yards from Brightman and his amateur army.

"Right flank, take cover," Brightman yelled.

Half of the soldiers raced fifty yards to the right, to the Lincoln Memorial. Some leapt up the steps and took cover behind the giant seated Lincoln. Others hid behind the memorial walls. A handful took a prone position by trees that decorated the nearby walkway, their firearms steadied and aimed.

Troller's eyes followed the path of the running soldiers. He grunted, turned his massive body, and stepped toward them.

"Left flank, take cover," Brightman yelled.

The remaining soldiers sped in the opposite direction to the World War II Memorial. They protected themselves behind the arches and stone structures.

Troller threw his head back and growled. Now focused on this second group, he changed direction and moved toward them.

In the center of the battlefield, Brightman pulled his shotgun up to his shoulder and aimed at the giant's midsection. By his side, Halendros flung his ammunition belt over his shoulder and lifted his automatic rifle, also taking aim. Nutley took two timid steps back, his eyes glued to the viewfinder of his video camera.

"Now!" Brightman said.

The two men opened fire.

Lead pelted the giant. He flinched, wiped his chest, then peered down at the men.

"I hope we can trust your guys," Brightman said as Troller took a step forward. "Right flank, attack!"

The right flank jumped out from their cover of the Lincoln Memorial. A fury of gunshots crackled through the air, relentlessly pounding the giant.

Troller let loose a piercing scream. He turned to face the blaze of bullets. Undeterred, he stomped a giant step toward the soldiers.

"Left flank, attack!"

The left flank jumped from their position in the World War II Memorial and opened fire.

Bullets assaulted Troller's back. He tried to reach behind him to bat away the annoyance.

Clearly confused, and not knowing who to attack, he stood in the Reflecting Pool as ammunition bombarded him from both sides. A moment later, he fell to one knee.

"Keep firing," Brightman called out as he lifted his shotgun and blasted another round at the giant's chest.

The assault continued. An endless barrage of gunfire lit the air like a Fourth of July fireworks display. Soon, a blanket of white smoke covered the battlefield.

With another monstrous scream, the giant leapt into the air. He landed with a crash, showering the area with a massive splash. He ran to his right, straight past the World War II Memorial and beyond the fighters stationed there.

Puzzled by the giant's move, Brightman watched and waited. "Hold your ground," he ordered the troops. It was clear by now that the small caliber weapons didn't even break the giant's skin.

The giant stopped at the Washington Monument. He reached up the sides of the structure with his massive hands and, pushing with his legs, shimmied himself up. He grabbed higher and pulled himself up again. He did this until he hung at the peak of the tower, five hundred feet off the ground.

With a great roar, he jumped. He flew through the air and landed with an earthquake-like force.

The monument swayed. Troller turned and rushed toward it. He grabbed it in his outstretched arms, braced his legs, and pushed.

The obelisk swayed more.

The giant grunted as he leaned into it. Finally, the monument began its descent. It toppled to the ground and shattered.

Troller stomped back toward the battlefield, shaking the ground. The Lincoln Memorial walls, crumbling around the twenty-foot-tall statue of the sixteenth president, forced the soldiers taking cover there to flee into the open field.

Troller reached down and snatched a fighter. A chorus of screams rang out as he pulled the man up to his face. He opened his massive mouth, raised the soldier into it, then clamped his ferocious teeth down across his victim's midsection.

A sickening crunch cut through the air.

Still holding the man's legs, Troller pulled, ripping the lower half away. He tossed the remains into the distance as he spit the upper half out.

As more troops scattered to avoid the crumbling structure, Troller, with one giant step or one long sweep of his arms herded everyone in the immediate area. He terrorized the army, picking men off one by one, crushing them into the ground, biting them in half, or flinging them a mile into the distance.

Through the smoke and dust, Brightman spotted an injured Halendros struggling to drag himself up a small section of steps amid the ruins of the Lincoln Memorial. He raced over to help.

"Grab his arm," he said to Nutley who was taking cover behind the statue of Lincoln.

They helped Halendros up the few remaining steps and laid the injured man down. Blood trickled from his mouth and streamed down his chin.

Brightman gritted his teeth as he looked at the injured man. For a moment, everything was silent. But the silence broke when Troller's massive hand came crashing down on top of Lincoln's head. The statue exploded like a ball of dust, disintegrating into the air.

Brightman looked around. They were trapped by walls, rocks, and debris on three sides, with the giant in front of them.

***

Eight year old Natanio Halendros crouched behind the bushes at the edge of the jungle. He checked left and right, making sure no one was around. Barefoot and tiptoeing, he ran swiftly to the hut that stood at the edge of the small military camp. He stopped and caught his breath. Listening for any sign his father was inside, he slinked along the outside of the small building.

The hustle bustle of rebel soldiers from the other side

of the hut made it difficult to hear any sound that might come from inside.

He continued to the end of the building and peeked around the corner as a jeep pulled up in front. Two more soldiers and another man, an American dressed in a dark suit with shiny black shoes and a fancy hat, stepped out of the jeep and entered the hut.

Natanio shifted a few more feet until he was under an open window. He lifted his head, getting his ear as close to the opening as he could, and listened closely.

His stomach fluttered with joy when he heard his father's voice.

His father spoke in English, the language he studied from the old book of American quotes he always seemed to have in hand.

It was difficult for Natanio to understand everything he heard. He could make out the words "freedom" and "liberty" and the phrase "have not yet begun to fight," but most of the other words he had never heard before.

He inched his head up to peek inside.

His father sat next to the American soldier that had saved him the day before. Both men were tied to their chairs. The new American, the well-dressed one, stood in front, talking to them. He spoke English much faster than his father did, and the words flew by too quickly for the boy to understand. But the tone was unmistakably mean.

Natanio lowered his head and thought hard about what he should do. What would his father do? The answer was easy. His father would be brave. His father would save them. So that is what he would do. Then they could go home. Maybe the American soldier would come. His father would like that, as he liked all things American. But there was a problem. He didn't know how to save the men. He slumped down against the wall to think, fidgeting with the rough-cut silver dollar hanging from a string around his neck.

"What are you doing here?" said a man in Spanish with an angry voice.

A chill shot through the boy's spine as he looked up with fear.

A rebel in combat greens stood at the corner of the hut and repeated his question.

Natanio jumped to his feet and raced toward the jungle, fleeing into the thick brush.

"Stop," the man called as he chased. "Come here."

The boy scurried through the jungle, jumping roots and ducking under branches, putting some distance between the man and himself. He ran until his legs began to tire, then stopped to catch his breath.

"Come here," the man called in the distance. He was getting closer.

Natanio searched for a place to hide. He spotted a small nook created by three large tree trunks and concealed by thick bushes. He lay down on his back, hidden in the thick ground cover.

The sun's rays fought through the canopy of leaves overhead and blasted down onto his face.

He shut his eyes tight.

As the man came nearer, the boy kept still.

A massive rumble shook the ground beneath him.

He threw his eyes open and the blinding sunlight beat down on his face. He squinted.

Troller stepped forward, eclipsing the sun.

Halendros, in the giant's shadow, turned his head and spit blood. He was injured, severely, and knew he was not going to escape. He looked at Brightman and Nutley next to him. They had a country to save. He thought about what his father would do. He would be brave. He would save the others.

He turned to Nutley, grabbing the video recorder and bringing his face an inch from the lens. "Tell the truth."

He struggled to his feet, then pulled his medallion over his head and hung it around Brightman's neck. He put his hand on the senator's shoulder and, with a nod, staggered down the steps.

"What are you doing?" Brightman said.

Halendros turned and balanced himself. "My only regret is that I have but one life to give for my country."

He grabbed his pistol, then dropped his holster, losing the extra weight.

With a sudden burst of adrenaline, he ran down the steps and through the giant's legs, yelling and firing his pistol like the Wild West cowboys his father used to tell him about in bedtime stories.

The giant shuffled above him, turning to track the fleeing man.

Halendros ran left, then right, zigzagging to prolong the inevitable as Troller swatted at him.

***

The next few seconds seemed to last an hour as Nutley stood, breathless, watching Halendros decoy the giant Democrat. His instinct was to film the action, but his arms hung heavy with dread and wouldn't lift.

Brightman grabbed the reporter's shirt and yanked him down the steps, pulling him to Halendros's car.

The senator slammed on the gas. The tires spun, shooting up dirt and grass until they caught traction. The truck sped forward, across the lot, and onto the road leading away from Constitution Gardens. Far enough away, and beyond Troller's danger zone, Brightman hit the brakes. The two men turned to watch the battlefield scene out the rear window.

The giant reached down and pulled up a small wriggling shape. He roared as he lifted up his prize.

Nutley shut his eyes tight to avoid seeing the horror in the distance. But it didn't help. The scene played itself out, in full gore, on the backs of his eyelids. A few seconds later, he felt the bumpy road underneath as the car started moving again.

In the distance, the giant went to work pulverizing the rest of the memorials and monuments in the area.

Nutley forced a swallow over the lump in his throat as his resilient guilt returned. By now, he was tired of it. Annoyed by it. Sick of it. Only now, it was stronger, reinforced by the heroics they were speeding away from.

"What now?" he said in a soft, somber voice.

"I'm going where I should have gone before," Brightman said. "McCleary Air Force Base."

CHAPTER 12

Brightman slammed the brakes and brought the truck to a screeching halt. He left the keys in the ignition and threw the door open. "You're on your own. Take your lies wherever you want."

"No," Nutley said, shaking his head. He held up his camera. "The truth needs to be told."

Brightman squinted, studying Nutley's face, unsure if the man was serious.

"The truth needs to be told," Nutley repeated. "And I'm going to tell it."

Brightman nodded slowly as he let the words sink. His gut told him Nutley was sincere. He pulled his pistol from his ankle holster and offered it.

Nutley hesitated, looking at the gun as if it would hiss and lunge any instant. He cautiously took it from Brightman's hand and secured it in his own.

"Safety's on," Brightman said. He slapped Nutley on the shoulder and got out of the car, then watched as it raced down the road and out of sight.

The senator approached the tall barbed-wire gate that protected the compound. A brick guard's booth stood off to the side and a young soldier with three stripes on his jacket sleeve stood at the door.

"I need to see Colonel Stupp," Brightman said.

"Strict orders he isn't to be disturbed." The soldier looked curiously at Brightman and then studied a photo that lay on the counter in the booth. He glanced up again. "Senator Brightman? I apologize, sir. Colonel Stupp has instructed me to call if you came." He picked up the phone that hung on the wall. "Senator Brightman is here," he said into the handset. He waited a moment, listening, then hung up and spoke to Brightman. "It'll just be a minute, Senator." He exited the booth and slid open the metal gate.

Brightman stepped inside and eyed the expansive compound from end to end. It was a ghost town. Amazing, there was a national emergency going on outside these gates and not one person was walking the grounds. The base should be at DEFCON 1, teeming with preparation, yet it was silent.

A jeep with two soldiers approached. "Hop in, Senator," the man in the passenger seat said. The soldiers drove Brightman to the far end of the complex and then escorted him to Stupp's office.

The smell of tobacco hung in the air. Cheap stuff, with an aroma like burnt flesh. Stupp stood behind his desk, gazing out the window into the distance.

Brightman spoke fast. "I don't know what you've heard or what you've seen, but there's a national emergency out there."

"Whoa," Stupp said, turning to Brightman, an unlit cigar off-center in his mouth. "Slow down. Have a seat."

"We don't have time to slow down." Brightman glanced at the two military men standing on each side of him, then back to Stupp. "Can we have a word, privately?"

Stupp nodded to the two soldiers. They left the room, closing the door behind them.

Brightman stepped behind the desk. "You know what's going on out there, don't you, Colonel?" he said, pointing outside. "The giants. They're all Democrats. Joros is behind it."

"Relax, Brightman. For starters, it's not colonel, it's general." He leaned his shoulder forward to show off his star.

Brightman hesitated. "Congratulations," he said, unconcerned considering the circumstances. "The giants. They're Democrats."

"Tell me about the other two. The scientist and the reporter. Where are they?"

"Gress and Nutley?" Brightman said, surprised Stupp would pay them any mind. "Forget them."

With his lips and teeth, the general shuffled the cigar to the center of his mouth and bit a piece from the end. He dropped the chunk out the side of his mouth and pointed to the lighter on his desk. "Would you mind?"

Brightman flipped the wad of wet tobacco from his shoe, grabbed the lighter, and lit Stupp's cigar.

The general took a long drag and blew out two thick rolling rings and then shifted the stogie to the side of his mouth. "I'm not sure exactly what you're doing here, but everything is under control."

"Under control?" Brightman said. He pointed out the window again. "The country is being destroyed and nobody's done a thing."

"I have strict orders," Stupp said. "And I intend to follow them." He leaned against the window sill and grimaced, hiding a groan deep in his throat, then quickly stood upright and shuffled his bottom.

"Orders? From who? And suddenly you're following orders?"

"Sorry, pal," Stupp said, ignoring the questions. "Manell. DiBraggo," he called.

The two soldiers returned to the room and stood at attention.

"Take the senator into custody," Stupp said.

The soldiers stepped to Brightman, one on each side, and grabbed his arms.

"What are you doing?" Brightman said, ripping free of the men's grips.

The soldiers pulled their guns, sticking the barrels against each of Brightman's temples.

"He got to you, didn't he?" Brightman said to Stupp. "Joros got to you."

Stupp scoffed.

"Let me see your ass," Brightman said. "You're branded aren't you?"

"Take him away," Stupp said.

"Move it," the soldiers said as they pushed Brightman out the door.

***

Nutley leaned forward to see all twenty stories of the MSM building through his windshield. He remained in the car for a moment, cycling through the events of the last few days in his mind. Led by Joros, the Democrats were destroying the country. Yet it was Brightman, and then Halendros, that had saved his life and spent every moment of the last few days trying to stop the giants.

He pounded his palms on the steering wheel. He had been a fool for too long. Determined to broadcast the truth, he got out of the car, slammed the door, and marched to the building.

With his head lowered so that he wouldn't be recognized, he focused on concealing his limp. It had become his defining characteristic in the last few years and was sure to get him instantly recognized. But as he focused on the evenness of his gait, he noticed something strange--the tingle in his leg was so faint he could barely notice it. In fact, maybe it was completely gone. It was hard to tell. Having grown so used to it, he forgot what it was like to have a non-tingling leg.

The lobby buzzed with action. Crowds of MSM employees darted everywhere, absorbed in their cell phone conversations, or walking and talking with coworkers.

"Get our West Coast affiliates on the line," a man said into his headset as he darted past. "If we get hit, we need backup."

"Where are the evacuation plans?" a man in a suit asked a security guard pushing a hand truck full of boxes. "If trouble strikes, we need to be ready. How's that basement shelter coming along?"

"On the six o'clock, let's lead with how the Republicans hate woman and children," a woman said to a younger man who struggled to keep up with her brisk steps. "Then we can segue into Brightman's involvement with the giants and tie it all together. He's still the most recognizable Republican. Let's make sure everyone knows he's the cause of this."

Having worked in the building for twenty years, Nutley

recognized all of the voices. But he kept his eyes on the floor and his goal in mind: edit the footage, air it for the country to see, and get out.

He worked his way through the crowd and into the stairwell, then bounded up the steps two at a time until he reached the fifth floor.

Although the editing department had abandoned this part of the building and moved to a lower floor months ago, much of the equipment remained in a room at the end of the hall. He slipped inside and closed the door behind him.

After copying his videos to the local drive of one of the computers in the room, he spent the next twenty minutes scanning, cutting, pasting, and organizing his footage. When he was finished, every place he had visited and every event he had witnessed over the course of the last two days made it into the condensed, unbiased, ten-minute segment. He copied the completed project to the digital tape in the computer's drive and ejected it.

With the editing finished, the story now needed to be broadcast. This part he couldn't do himself. A channel needed to be hijacked and the planned programming overridden. For that, he had to be in the control room and he needed the technical know-how. He needed to find Billy. If there was anyone in this building that could get the job done, and that he could trust, his ex-assistant was the guy. Sure, their last meeting was awkward, but when the chips were down, he knew he could still count on his protégé. He called Billy's extension and told him to come to the old editing room on the fifth floor.

"I have something I need aired," Nutley said when

Billy arrived.

"What are you talking about? And what are you doing here?"

Nutley held the tape up. "You know how to get this broadcasted. The country has to see it."

"Sorry, but I'm a reporter now," Billy said. "No more behind-the-scenes work for me. When you got canned, I got promoted."

"Fine. You want the biggest story you'll ever get? It's yours. These giants that are destroying everything, the Democrats are behind it all." He pointed to the tape in his hand. "It's all here. We have to air this and let the country see it. It'll be the biggest story ever reported."

"Sorry," Billy said before turning to leave. "I don't need your help anymore."

As Billy turned toward the door, Nutley could only think of one way to stop him. He pulled the pistol Brightman had given him and cocked the hammer.

The sound of the metal click stopped Billy in his tracks. He turned back around slowly, eyed the gun in Nutley's hand, and raised his arms above his head.

**

Brightman sat on the floor in the corner and scanned the room for the thousandth time. There was no way out. No windows and only one door, which was blocked by Manell and DiBraggo, who kept their hands on their weapons. They didn't move until there was a knock on the door, and Stupp entered. A small metal case hung by a strap from the crook of the General's elbow.

Brightman jumped to his feet. "Why did you do it? Why did you let Joros get to you?"

Stupp ignored the questions and walked to the other side of the room where he set the metal case down on a small table.

"What about your country?" Brightman said. "What about loyalty?"

"Don't talk to me about loyalty," Stupp said, whipping around. "The last time you had a chance to prove your loyalty, I lost these." He raised his stumps in the air.

Brightman stared at the stumps with disdain. It was the perfect reminder that he had betrayed the trust of his friend, his men, and his country. The fact that he had no control over it, that he was drugged with truth serum, was of little consolation. It may have been more than twenty years ago, but it was a wound even time couldn't heal.

"You know," Stupp said as he itched his cheek with his stump, "when I lost my hands, I thought it was the end of my time in the Air Force." A snarl settled on his face. "But it was even worse than that. They kept me around for pity. It took them twenty years to finally put me in charge here, after they all but shut the place down."

"So what now? You get revenge for anger you've been hiding for twenty years?"

"Revenge? No. I get what I finally deserve. A promotion to general."

"In exchange for capturing me, you make general. Is that the deal? Is that what Joros traded you?"

Stupp remained silent.

"He's the one who cut off your hands," Brightman

said.

"Bygones are bygones. Now tell me where Gress and Nutley are. We don't need them complicating things."

Gress may have lost his mind, but Brightman knew he was still the only man alive who had any chance of finding an antidote for the giants. As slim as that chance was, he wouldn't utter a word about the doctor's whereabouts. Nutley, in the process of getting the truth to the American people, needed protection just as much.

"They're dead," Brightman said.

Stupp smiled. He tilted his head slightly to the side and squinted. "You know I don't believe that for a minute."

He jammed his stump into the latch on the metal case, popping the top open. After balancing the box on his forearm, he propped it up to show the contents to Brightman. "I think you know what this is."

Brightman's stomach dropped when he saw the needle-- truth serum.

Stupp nodded to Manell and DiBraggo and the two soldiers grabbed Brightman's arms. The senator struggled but the men overpowered him.

Stupp dropped his head and took the syringe from the case, sideways, into his mouth. As the guards held the prisoner still, Stupp lowered his head and guided the needle into Brightman's shoulder. He pressed the bottom of the syringe with his forearm.

Heat from the serum flooded Brightman's arm.

The soldiers loosened their grips and eased the senator into a chair by the wall as he slid into a state of naive candidness.

Stupp turned and spit the syringe onto the floor. "Now,"

he said, turning back to Brightman, "tell me where the others are."

***

"You know what to do," Nutley said to Billy. He nodded to a row of monitors and kept his gun pointed at his ex-assistant. He had warmed considerably to the deadly hunk of steel in his grip and was strangely comfortable with it as he liberally waved it around.

Billy watched his captor through the corner of his eye as he put the tape in the drive and logged on. He concentrated at the job on hand, looking up only when the door opened and three MSM employees entered the room.

"What is he doing here?" a man said, pointing at Nutley.

Nutley rushed over to the men with his gun arm outstretched. Two of them froze in fear, but the third turned to run. Nutley lunged forward and grabbed the man by the shirt, dragging him back into the room and slamming the door. "Over there. Move it," he demanded, pointing to a table in the corner.

"What's taking so long?" he asked Billy. It was only a matter of time before more people started coming.

"I'm trying," Billy said. "I need to find an open channel, but I'm getting nothing. There must be networks down all over the city."

A moment later, two more employees entered the room. Again, Nutley used the threat of his firearm to make the men join the others.

He leaned against a table, keeping an eye on his growing group of captives. His confidence increased every time he saw the fear spread across the their faces. This was getting easier by the minute. The fact that he had never fired a gun in his life, let alone held one, didn't matter a bit. He was in control. As far they were concerned, he was a crazy, gun-wielding maniac, and they were clearly terrified. He could do this all day.

When the door opened a third time, Nutley jumped to meet the visitors, but he stopped in his tracks when Joros entered into the room, followed by his two thugs.

Nutley stepped back. His hand quivered as he pointed the gun at Joros a mere ten feet away. There was no fear in Joros's eyes. He was not like the others.

Suddenly, the firearm failed to bring Nutley confidence. Suddenly, it mattered that he had never fired a gun. It mattered that he had never even held one.

An expressionless Joros moved forward again.

Nutley took another step back, his hand still shaking.

Joros, staring coldly, came forward again.

Nutley held his ground, but his hand trembled wildly, and he needed his other hand to help steady the gun.

"Senator Brightman said you would be here." Joros lifted his hand slowly and grabbed the barrel of the shaking gun, pushing it aside.

Nutley melted, and let the gun slip easily into Joros's grip.

Joros walked to Billy's computer and removed the digital tape. He dropped it on the linoleum floor and dug the heel of his polished black shoe into it, cracking and grinding it into pieces.

***

Pushed from behind, Nutley's head snapped back as he stumbled across the room and crashed into the wall on the far end.

"You got company," Stupp said before slamming the door shut.

Nutley regained his balance, saw Brightman, and lowered himself on the floor next to the senator. He glanced over at the two soldiers standing guard.

Nutley spoke softly to Brightman. "I guess you didn't find what you were looking for."

"Nope," Brightman said, a blank expression sculpted on his face. "You didn't get the truth out?"

"Nope," Nutley said. "So, what do we do now?"

Brightman shrugged. "There's nothing we can do."

Nutley stared straight ahead, not wanting to look at the senator. What was Brightman thinking? Was he thinking that Nutley, complicit with the Democrats for so long, brought all this about? Maybe he was thinking how things would be different if he had won the election four years ago--the election he would have won had it not been for the lies. The damn lies. Nutley knew they were lies but it didn't matter at the time. The means justified the ends. Wasn't that all that mattered? And what about Halendros? The man gave his life for his country--for the truth.

With a deep sigh, and a deeper feeling of shame, Nutley put his hands in his pockets and shuddered himself. His fingers touched something in his pocket. He wrapped his hand around it--a vial he had taken from Gress's lab.

The door opened and Joros entered the room. "Good

evening, gentlemen. I wanted to come and say farewell."

"Like we care where you're going?" Nutley said.

Joros chuckled. "I'm not going anywhere. But you didn't think you were getting out of here alive, did you?" He stepped forward and squatted in front of Brightman. "I seem to remember, some years ago, you saying something about a governing document. How this isn't the kind of country you can just walk into and take control of." He smirked, then stood and walked to the door. "Soon, I will have total control of this government and, with the country in dire need of rebuilding, President Puppit will implement my vision for America Tomorrow, he will address the nation and explain my plans for rebuilding the country."

The two prisoners sat silent as Joros turned and left the room.

After making sure the guards weren't looking, Nutley pulled the vial out of his pocket and hid it in his palm. "I took this from Gress's lab the other day," he said in a whisper "What do you think would happen if I took it. Would I grow big? Maybe I could break us out of here."

"I think this stuff has caused enough problems," Brightman whispered back. "Just put it away."

Nutley grabbed the vial tighter. He had to try something. He poured the potion into his mouth.

"What are you doing?" Brightman said, grabbing Nutley's arm to try and stop him.

But it was too late. He had swallowed the liquid.

The two men stared at each other, waiting and watching.

"Do you feel anything?" Brightman whispered.

"Nothing," Nutley said. He stood and paced as he waited, focusing on himself, trying to notice if he felt even the slightest bit different.

"What are you doing?" DiBraggo said. "Sit down."

In an instant, a swift icy chill swept Nutley's body. He stumbled and fell to the floor. The cold turned to hot. The hot turned back to cold. He moaned as shooting pains ran through his body.

"Holy crap," DiBraggo said. "I'm getting Stupp."

"You're not leaving me here to take the blame for this," Manell said.

The two men left the room together, locking the door behind them.

As suddenly as Nutley's pains had come, they disappeared just as quick. He wiped his face and rested on one knee. After a few deep breaths, he stood. "That felt weird."

Brightman's jaw dropped. He stared with wide eyes and a white face.

"Why are you looking at me like that?" Nutley said. "What happened?" He ran his hands over his face, feeling for defects. What did he look like? What kind of monster had he become? "What happened?" he shouted.

The door opened and Stupp stepped into the room with the two soldiers. The general took one look at Nutley and froze, then staggered back a step.

Nutley ran his hands over his face again, trying to feel the hideousness the others were seeing.

Stupp took a tentative step forward. He leaned in and studied Nutley curiously. A grin worked its way onto the general's face, followed by a look of pure jubilation. He sheepishly stepped back, then stood straight and snapped off a handless salute to the man that stood before him.

Nutley wasn't sure what the other men in the room were looking at, but he clearly no longer looked like himself, and he knew enough to play along. He returned Stupp's salute. "At ease," he said in the most commanding voice he could muster.

"President Reagan, sir," Brightman said deliberately, "I think we are going to be late for our plane if we don't leave now."

President Reagan? Nutley hesitated as Brightman's words sunk in. "Uh, yes, you're right, Senator. General, please excuse us."

"I'm sorry, Mr. President," Stupp said, "but I'm supposed to keep everyone here. I'm under direct orders."

Nutley stepped confidently toward Stupp. He straightened the general's tie and rested his hand on the man's shoulder. He chuckled lightly. "Well," he said, "there you go again."

He gave the general a reassuring pat and then stepped past him and out of the room.

***

"This way," Brightman said, racing through the halls as a Reagan-like Nutley followed. He burst out the door to the rear of the compound.

Dozens of mountainous piles of disassembled fighter jets, tanks, and other military equipment laid scattered around the otherwise open field. In the distance, an old hangar stood alone.

Brightman raced to the hangar and kicked in the entrance door. A single FT-15 sat in the center. With his eyes closed, he slowly ran his hand over its steel exterior, breathing deep as the cold metal tantalized his fingertips. Excitement and pride flushed through him as he reunited with his old friend.

"Hurry," Nutley said. "They're coming."

Brightman turned to find a crowd of soldiers running across the compound. He grabbed a rolling ladder and placed it next to the cockpit. "Get in," he said to Nutley. "Back seat."

He rushed to the rear of the hangar and pulled the lever to open the bay's hydraulic door, then jumped up the ladder and into the front seat. With the flip of a switch he closed the cockpit glass, then started the plane and taxied out of the hangar.

"Hold on," he called back to Nutley, advancing the power lever.

The afterburners roared as the plane accelerated. Seconds later, it floated off the ground, lifting smoothly into the air.

He headed north, toward D.C. "It shouldn't be too hard to find him," he called back to Nutley. "And it should be just as easy to hit him."

He touched the various controls and gauges, refamiliarizing himself with the weapons system--two missiles and a full load of 30-millimeter cannons. There was no way Troller could withstand this kind of firepower. And once Troller was taken care of, it was simply a matter of reloading and finding the rest of the giants. It wouldn't be easy, it wouldn't be quick, but it was the only way to get the job done.

He admired the view of the clear late-afternoon sky in

front of him. If he could, he would stay up here, gliding between the earth and the clouds forever. His reverie ended, however, when Troller's head appeared over the horizon.

Adrenaline surged through the pilot. Poised for battle, he squeezed the throttle lever tighter. He lowered the craft's nose, and powered forward.

The jet screamed, jumping through the air just above the rooflines as it zeroed in on the giant.

Troller looked up when he spotted the plane. He dropped two cars he was playing with and turned to square himself with the approaching fighter.

Brightman kept the throttle forward, heading straight for the giant. As he neared his target, he unleashed cannon fire. A stream of 30-millimeter shells floated through the air and pounded the giant's chest.

Troller roared as they ricocheted off him.

Brightman pulled back, lifting the plane's nose and navigating over the giant's head.

"Did we get him?" Nutley asked.

"Bounced off him like BBs," Brightman said. "It's time for the heavy stuff." He circled around in a long arching loop, putting some distance between himself and the giant, and prepared for another run. He throttled forward toward Troller again, took aim, and locked in.

The system beeped.

He pulled the trigger.

The starboard air-to-air missile leapt off the wing. A plume of white smoke trailed as it screeched toward the Democrat.

The giant tracked the missile, raised his arm, and batted it out of the sky. It tumbled, end over end, and exploded when it hit the ground a half-mile away.

"Well?" Nutley said.

Brightman clenched his jaw. He shook his head slowly. "Swatted it away like a fly." There was one missile left and he couldn't let Troller see this one coming. He pointed the fighter's nose into the air and accelerated into the sky, then circled back and flew at the giant from behind.

He took aim and locked in.

But Troller turned and lunged at the plane. His massive fingers grazed the rear.

Brightman lost control.

The plane flew into a tailspin and headed toward the Potomac.

"Eject! Eject! Eject!" Brightman reached for the release under the seat, yanked it, and catapulted out of the craft.

He tumbled through the air until his parachute opened. As he drifted down, he watched Troller wading into the river, far upstream, chasing after the jet.

Not far away, Nutley, also safely ejected, descended into the river with him.

CHAPTER 13

The two men swam to shore and found cover in an alcove lined with rocks and small trees.

Troller waded into the Potomac and retrieved the disabled aircraft. Like a troubled child playing with a captured bug, he pulled off the wings, banged it, shook it, and squeezed it. After growing disinterested, he tossed its smoldering fuselage to the side and then hunched over and scanned the water for the two men. Unable to find them, he roared with frustration and bounded into the distance.

"Now what?" Nutley said.

Brightman wiped water off his face and turned to Nutley. His eyes widened with surprise when he looked at the reporter.

"What?" Nutley said. "What is it now?" He frantically rubbed his hands over his face.

"Nothing," Brightman said. "The potion wore off. You're you again, that's all. Just caught me by surprise."

"Oh," Nutley said with relief, dropping his hands to his sides. He strolled back to the edge of the water and, with shoulders slumped, gazed into the distance across the river.

Brightman left him alone and found a large rock to sit on. He tried to piece together what the next few days, months, and years would look like. Soon, the country would be ravaged beyond recognition. Worse still, Joros, pulling Puppit's strings, sat waiting to rebuild it.

He sat a while longer, until his attention was caught by Nutley talking to himself and gesturing with his hands as he looked out across the river. Intrigued, Brightman approached him. As he got nearer, Nutley's words became clearer.

"*Tear* down that wall," Nutley said to himself. He repeated it, relocating the emphasis. "Tear down *that* wall." He motioned with his hands. "Tear down that *wall.*"

"It's 'tear down *this* wall,'" Brightman said.

Nutley turned, startled. "I was just, um ... uh ..."

Brightman grinned and gave his best Reagan impression. "Tear down this wall."

Nutley nodded an impressed approval. "Tear down this wall," he tried.

"Stronger," Brightman said. "More commanding. But soothing ... Tear down. Like that."

"Tear down ... ," Nutley said before his voice trailed off.

"Better. But put more feeling into it. Remember, there was nothing aloof about him."

"Tear down," Nutley started. "No wait ... tear down ... tear ... tear down this wall."

"Good," Brightman said.

The two men laughed, trading impressions a little while longer before Nutley turned serious. "What do we do now?"

"There's nothing we can do," Brightman said. He hung his head and let out a long sigh. "It's over. America as we know it is over."

The men took a seat on some rocks. Minutes passed

as they sat in silence. Finally, with determination in his voice, Nutley spoke. "We need to get the truth out."

Brightman gave a frustrated, disparaging laugh. "It's over."

"No," Nutley said. "Doesn't the country deserve to know the truth? What about all those people back at the National Mall? What about Halendros?"

Brightman nodded slowly as he thought about the patriots who had fought the giant. But he thought mostly of Halendros, of the sacrifice he had made, just as his father so many years earlier.

"You're right. The people deserve the truth. But who's going to tell it? Me? You? Who would listen to us? At this point we would need Puppit to come clean at tomorrow's press conference, and I don't think that's going to happen."

Nutley flashed a mischievous smile. "You never know."

Brightman laughed off the ridiculous comment. "Puppit tell the truth? That'll be the day."

"Would this help?" Nutley pulled a syringe from his pocket and dangled it in front of him.

"Truth serum?" Brightman stared in amazement. "Where did you get that?"

"It was just lying on the floor in the room we were in at McCleary."

A glimmer of hope seeded itself as Brightman eyed the needle. "But it's not full."

Nutley held it up to get an accurate reading through the plastic tube. "No, it's about a quarter full. You think it's enough?"

Brightman pictured the president in his mind. Tall and lanky. Kind of scrawny. Not much muscle. "He couldn't weigh more than ninety-nine pounds wet." He nodded. "I think that might do it."

"It's a long shot," Nutley said.

"Yeah, but it's our only shot."

The two men huddled together and set out the details of their plan.

***

As if it were a winning lottery ticket, Brightman checked and double checked that the syringe was secure in the inside pocket of his coat. They only had one chance, and there was no margin for error.

He turned to the passenger side window to hide his face as Nutley pulled up to the White House gate to present his press pass. The security guard waved them forward and Nutley parked. He flashed his ID card at the next check point and the two men strolled past a row of Secret Service agents, through a body scan, across the lobby, and into the press room.

The room buzzed with chatter from scattered cliques of journalists, all anxious for the president's momentous speech. Nutley headed to the back of the room.

Brightman, his eyes locked on the floor and hoping no one would recognize him, navigated to the front and took a seat directly in front of the podium.

Soon, the president would enter and, as usual, spend some time giving high fives and grabbing accolades from his admirers. Brightman would be center of the mix. Amidst the chaos, Puppit might not even feel the needle. But even if he did, it would be too late.

He took a deep breath. A small chuckle slipped out. He had been under the influence of the serum twice. Both times he knew it was happening, and both times he succumbed to it anyway. The weak-minded president wouldn't even know it was coming, and surely stood no chance.

"Pomp and Circumstance" crescendoed in the background. The side door opened and Puppit entered the room. His adoring fans rushed to him like young girls to their heartthrob, reaching out for a handshake, a high five, or a fist bump.

Brightman kept the syringe hidden under his cupped hand as he tried to squeeze his way toward the front of the crowd. But he had underestimated the tenacity of the fans' adulation, and couldn't get past the second row. He pushed hard with his one free hand, struggling to wedge himself between two reporters. By accident, he came cheek to cheek with one of them. He quickly shot his head down, but it was too late. The reporter had recognized him.

"What is Brightman doing here?" the reporter said, stepping back from the crowd. The words were devoured by the commotion, but he promptly repeated them. A few others took notice and echoed the question.

A moment later, the music stopped. Silence set in and all eyes fell on Brightman. As two Secret Service agents hurried to the scene and grabbed him, he hid the syringe in his cupped hand, making sure not jab himself with the needle.

"Clear away," the president said. "Everyone, take your seats." He stepped in front of Brightman.

"How ironic you should show up. I was just about to tell the good people of the country what a big role you and your Republican colleagues have played in the events of the last few days. I would ask you to tell them yourself, but they probably wouldn't believe you."

He looked around the room, pausing for dramatic effect. "Unless, of course, we gave you some truth serum."

The crowd joined in laughter at the president's mockery. As the Secret Service agents giggled, Brightman felt their grip on his right arm loosen just a bit.

To keep Puppit off guard, he laughed along with the joke. Then, in one swift motion, he yanked his arm from the agent's control, opened his hand as it flew toward Puppit, and plunged the syringe into the president's shoulder.

The agents jumped on Brightman, crushing him on the floor underneath them.

"He stabbed the president!" someone shouted.

"Assassin!" someone else yelled.

Panic ensued. A flurry of camera flashes lit the room. Yelling and shouting morphed into a single, deep rumble that saturated the air. Every reporter raced to the president as Secret Service agents pushed them away.

"The president is fine," Nutley yelled from the back of the room. "It's only truth serum."

The room quieted as Nutley continued. "Mr. President, would you like to say a few words about what has really happened these last few days?"

The president enjoyed an easy smile. "Well, Joros and I, we find this giant, right? It's Troller, you see--"

The side door burst open. "No," Joros screamed as he raced into the room. "Stop talking. He doesn't know what he's saying. He's been drugged by that maniac." He pointed to Brightman on the floor, covered by the agents.

The room quieted. From the middle of the crowd, a lone voice spoke. "Let's hear what the president has to say."

"No," Joros said. "The president needs medical attention." He grabbed Puppit by the arm. "Let's go."

Puppit pulled his arm free. "No. I really feel like talking."

"Yeah, let's hear him," a voice from the crowd said. Another agreed. Then another.

Collectively, the mass of reporters blocked Joros, pushing him backward as the president spoke.

"Whatever he says, it's all lies," Joros said as he tried, unsuccessfully, to force his way through the crowd. "You want the truth? That's the truth. There." He pointed to the teleprompter. "Start that stupid thing. I'll read it myself."

"So, we find Troller," the president continued, "and he's like fifty ... fifty-seven feet tall." He raised his hands into the air, stumbled back a step, and then straightened himself out before continuing. "So, we figure, what if all the Democrats could be giants." He wobbled to the left, wobbled to the right, and then steadied himself. "We could destroy this place. You know what I mean? Just totally transform it. Fundamentally. Move it forward."

He dropped his head. When he lifted it again, he looked out across the crowd and smiled. He teetered, tottered, and then fell backwards. He hit the ground with a thud and the room fell silent.

The president's doctor rushed to kneel next to the fallen chief executive, feeling for the pulse in his neck.

"Is he dead?" someone called out.

***

The doctor propped Puppit up against the podium and the president's head fell limp to the side. His eyes, bloodshot and glassy, as in a drug-induced haze, stared straight ahead without focus. A line of drool hung from his open mouth. The doctor began a battery of basic tests on the stupefied president.

"Do you see now?" Brightman said, breaking the hush that hung over the room. "Puppit and Joros are behind the giants. You heard it from the president himself."

"How do we know this isn't some kind of trick?" a reporter said.

"Yeah, he's still our president," said another. "We're not going to just abandon him because of one thing he said, which may or may not even be true."

The room grew louder as each reporter voiced a stronger, more forceful allegiance to the president.

Brightman sighed. He was up against something every bit as devastating as fifty-foot-tall monsters--media bias. Seeing the truth with their own eyes, and hearing it with their own ears, meant nothing. They had been trained their entire careers to ignore the truth. They had turned denial into art, deception into science, and outright lying into sport.

Nutley marched to the podium and tapped the microphone. "Man crushes."

The room quieted and focused on the speaker.

"That's what I'm hearing," Nutley said. "All this commotion. It's the result, the manifestations, of your man crushes."

A murmur arose. "What are you talking about?" a

reporter said.

"That's nonsense," said another.

The reporters joined together, jeering and scoffing at Nutley's allegation.

"I know what's really going on in your mind right now," Nutley said. "I felt it too. You feel betrayed. Confused. Lied to. Lost. For four years now, it's been building. I understand."

"That's ridiculous," a chorus of voices yelled out.

"I didn't want to believe it either. But look at yourselves. You're all a mess."

Nutley summoned Rob Roberts to the podium. "How long have you been drooling like this?"

Roberts, the front of his shirt saturated with saliva, blushed and wiped a slobbering drip from his chin. "About four--" he gagged and drooled another stream. "About four years, I guess."

"Right," said Nutley. "Since the last election. That's the man crush. Stevens, where are you?"

Steve Stevens worked his way through the crowd, scratching profusely as he approached the podium. "This itching, it's been driving me crazy." He untucked his shirt from his pants and attacked his belly with his fingernails.

"Since Puppit's been president," said Nutley. "Right?"

Stevens nodded.

"Man crush."

Mike Michaels stepped forward. "Hab aboob a gloop, mao mao?"

"Yes," Nutley said. "Your man crush."

"Well, what do we do?" said Will Williams, stepping through the crowd in just his boxers and black dress socks.

"Trust yourself. Not him," Nutley said, pointing to the drooling, babbling president at the base of the podium. "Know what you believe. Know why you became a journalist in the first place. Get that renegade spirit back."

The crowd slowly closed in around Nutley.

Roberts stepped up to him behind the podium. Nutley closed his eyes and laid his hands on the man's shoulders. "Tell the truth," he said, gently pushing him back.

Roberts balanced himself, then stood silent and still. He smacked his lips. "I'm not drooling." He smiled and wiped his chin. "It's dry."

Roberts stepped away and Stevens took his place. Nutley laid his hands on the man's shoulders. "Tell the truth."

Stevens's eyes widened with delight. "I'm not itching."

One by one, the reporters approached Nutley to be ridded of their ailments.

Brightman turned his attention to the doctor still tending to the president at the base of the podium. Although relieved he wasn't an assassin, he couldn't understand what had gone wrong. Why did Puppit have such a horrible reaction to the serum? He, himself, had been given the truth serum twice and nothing like this had happened.

Then it hit him. Nothing like this had happened because he wasn't a Democrat.

"The truth," he yelled. "It's poison to a Democrat!"

The room hushed.

"It's like kryptonite to Superman. Like garlic to a vampire."

"That means we can stop the giants with it," Nutley said.

A jubilant clamor arose as the crowd wondered aloud about the possibility of stopping the giants with truth serum.

Brightman approached the president's doctor. "Doc, can you get truth serum? We need a lot of it."

"Yes. Sodium Pentothal," the doctor said. "I can get all we need at the hospital down the road." He adjusted the president, making sure he was propped up securely against the podium. "Somebody watch him," he said as he raced out of the room.

Puppit, still streaming drool from his mouth, slid sideways and hunched over onto the floor.

Brightman approached the agent who had restrained him earlier. "I need you to get Marine One ready for me. Then find out where the giant is."

"I'm on it, Senator," the agent said, running out the door.

Nutley finished ushering out the reporters who were now on their way to report the truth, then stepped over Puppit and joined Brightman.

The two men headed for Marine One.

CHAPTER 14

The ambulance skidded to a stop just outside the White House helipad. The president's doctor jumped out of the driver's seat and pulled open the back doors, revealing two stacks of four boxes each. The side of each box was stamped "Sodium Pentothal. 50mL. Quantity 500."

"This is everything they had," the doctor said.

Brightman pulled a box to the ground and ripped the top open. He grabbed one of the clear plastic bags and cradled it in his hand. "This should to do it. Let's get it loaded."

After the boxes were loaded onto the chopper, Nutley climbed in to the rear of the craft with them. Brightman settled into the pilot's seat and put the headset on. He leaned on the throttle, lifting the helicopter into the air. When he cleared the White House, he pulled back on the controls, sending the craft forward.

"This is Marine One," he said into the mouthpiece. "Can I get a read on the giant?"

"He's across the Anacostia," the agent said over the radio. "Fly south and you should see him in no time."

Brightman turned the chopper and headed south. He powered forward, bringing the craft up to maximum speed. A moment later, Troller's head came into view over a row of buildings.

The giant romped through the street, ripping at power lines, and poking holes into apartment windows with his massive index finger. But as the chopper approached, he heard it and turned to track it.

Brightman took the craft into a sharp right turn, behind a row of tall buildings. He pulled up, above the giant's head, and came around behind him.

Troller turned and spotted the craft. He roared. The monstrous sound rippled through the air, rattling the copter.

Brightman steadied the craft, then hovered a dozen yards directly above Troller's head. The giant's stubby neck prevented him from looking up, making it the safest place to be.

"I'm going to get nice and close," Brightman called to Nutley, screaming over the whirring of the blades. "When you get a clear shot, let it fly."

Troller spun, trying to look up. He used the surrounding buildings for balance, resting his tremendous hands on the chimneys, which he knocked over, and the rooftops, which he collapsed.

"Here we go," Brightman said. He put the nose down and dropped lower, hovering a few yards above the giant's head.

Troller leaned back to looked up, his six-foot-wide canyon of a mouth opened wide.

"Now!" Brightman said.

Nutley, secured to the inside of the helicopter with a nylon strap, leaned out the open door. He squeezed a plastic bag. It popped. Serum shot into Troller's mouth. Nutley worked fast, emptying one bag after another until Troller tasted the liquid.

The giant coughed. Massive wads of phlegm shot up, hitting the underside of the helicopter and sticking to it.

The chopper spun as the extra weight unbalanced it and Brightman fought to keep it straight.

Nutley, drenched in the Democrat's slimy spit, leaned out again and continued throwing bags of serum on the Democrat. The plastic packets pummeled the giant's face, popping open and drenching him.

Troller hunched over, trying to avoid the falling bags. He reached down, pulled a lamppost out of the ground, and flung it into the air, over his head.

Brightman throttled forward to avoid the lamppost but it grazed the tail. The chopper careened out of control. Brightman maneuvered the twisting craft. "We're coming in hard," he called back to Nutley. They spun wildly, crashing down on a nearby rooftop. Flames engulfed the engine.

The men jumped out of the machine and raced to the other side of the roof. Behind them, the copter exploded. In front of them, stood Troller.

The giant shook his head and rubbed his tongue. He stumbled, bracing himself against the surrounding buildings, then stopped and stood motionless. A crackling sound pierced the air as his head expanded. His eyes bulged. With a pop, his left eye shot from its socket and careened toward Brightman.

Brightman dove, avoiding the speeding white projectile.

It rolled across the rooftop and fell off the other end.

The right eye followed, shooting clear across the

building.

The giant's head continued to grow as snaps and rips reverberated through the air. He clasped his hands against the sides of his head. He grunted and groaned, then roared.

BOOM!

The giant fell into the street with an enormous crash.

A peaceful silence followed.

Moments later, the silence was broken by the pitter-patter of Democrat brain and skull raining down.

***

*** BREAKING NEWS ***

*** BILLY SAMPLE REPORTING ***

*** BEGIN OFFICIAL TRANSCRIPT ***

BILLY SAMPLE: Billy Sample, reporting for MSM with great news for America. All across the land, from sea to shining sea, giant Democrats are dropping like incredibly large flies.

Our running count has the number at twelve. Twelve Democrats down. Hold on. Wait a minute. I've just received word that number thirteen is practically in the bag. Let's pick up the action in San Francisco.

(BEGIN LIVE FEED FROM SAN FRANCISCO, CA)

SAN FRANCISCO COMMENTATOR: I'm here at the Golden Gate Bridge and there is the giant Democrat--Senator Cratt, we believe--making his way across the bridge.

The Marin County and San Francisco fire departments have just arrived and the fire trucks are getting out their hoses now. I'm told that the water is laced with truth serum.

They're pounding him with truth serum from the hoses now, just bombarding him with a steady stream from both sides. The giant is caught in the middle with no place to turn.

I can't believe what I'm seeing here. The giant's head is getting bigger. It's growing before my very eyes. It's actually expanding.

He's climbing up the suspension cables, now. The Democrat is trying desperately to escape the truth--the truth serum. It looks like that is as high as he can get, but it's just not high enough. The fire departments are soaking him again.

He's slipping. He's losing his balance. And there he goes into the bay. What a splash! He just toppled right over, off the cables, and into the water. He's sinking. It's real quiet all of a sudden and--what is that? Some sort of bubbling. If you look where the giant fell, there is a flurry of bubbles coming to the surface.

(MASSIVE EXPLOSION)

Oh my goodness! He exploded. I don't know if you got that on tape. Like a nuke detonating under water. Just a massive explosion. It's a good thing we have our ponchos on because it's raining down now. Water everywhere. And it looks like solid chunks in addition to the water. That can only be, I assume, pieces of Senator Cratt's brain. That giant head exploded and is falling on us now. Pretty gross, really.

(END LIVE FEED FROM SAN FRANCISCO, CA)

BILLY SAMPLE: And there you have it. Thirteen Democrats down and--hold on--I'm getting word Texas is on the verge of taking down another. Apparently, a giant Democrat has been trapped in the Houston Astrodome and--we have video of this? Okay, let's stream that in.

(BEGIN LIVE FEED FROM HOUSTON, TX)

HOUSTON COMMENTATOR: I'm outside the Astrodome and, to be honest, I don't know how he got in there, but a giant Democrat-- we believe it is Senator Dingers--is inside the stadium. From what I understand, a truth serum mist is being pumped inside though the air conditioning vents.

(MASSIVE EXPLOSION)

Holy Cow! Did you see that? Something just blew a hole in the Astrodome's roof. Well, if the earlier reports of the exploding Democrat heads are accurate, I'm going to take a guess and say Dingers's head exploded and shot clear through the dome. I think these pieces falling from the sky support that theory.

(END LIVE FEED FROM HOUSTON, TX)

BILLY SAMPLE: So the total is now fourteen Democrats down.

Okay, wait a minute, another update coming in. It seems we have some action in the wide-open space of the Iowa cornfields. Two Democrats there. Crop dusters have been loaded with truth serum and are taking care of them. That would make fifteen and sixteen. So, the number now is sixteen Democrats down and--wait, we've got more coming.

Looks like we have another in Florida. Number seventeen.

Okay, now we've got eighteen in Kansas.

Seattle--nineteen.

Boise--twenty.

America is on a roll.

A great day for America.

*** END TRANSCRIPT ***

CHAPTER 15

"On the air in three, two, one." The cameraman's bony index finger pointed to Nutley as the "On Air" sign lit up.

Nutley looked into camera number one. "The truth will set you free, but first it will make you miserable--James A. Garfield." He turned to camera two. "Thanks for joining me for the first edition of True Talk where we ask the tough questions and won't stop until we get to the truth. "A lot has happened over the last few days and, as horrifying an experience as it's been, I think there's been a little bit of a silver lining. We have certainly seen the misery James Garfield spoke of and I'd like to take some time to discuss the many ways it has set us free.

"But first, we have a very special guest tonight. Since there will be so much to talk about, let's not waste any time. Ladies and gentlemen, please welcome the man who saved the country, Senator Bart Brightman."

Applause erupted as the audience rose to their feet. Hoots and hollers echoed throughout the room. Brightman entered the set, waved to the crowd, and took a seat next to the host.

Nutley leaned in to welcome the senator, but the greeting was drowned out by the crowd's continued adulation. The two men waited until the noise died down.

"Whew," Nutley said. "That was some welcome."

"Yes," Brightman said, turning to the audience. "Thank you for that."

Applause rose again. "Thank you," someone from the

audience shouted. "We love you," yelled another.

"You know," Nutley said when the room quieted, "so much has happened these past few days and you were right in the middle of it all. Now, as everyone knows, you did not run for re-election and so, pretty soon, you are going to be out of public service for the first time in, really, your entire life. How are you going to handle that?"

"With a fishing pole and a beer," Brightman said. He laughed, and the audience laughed with him. "Seriously though, you're right, I've always been in public service. But you know, when we were knee deep in this struggle with the Democrats, we met an incredible American, Natanio Halendros."

"Brave man," Nutley said.

"Absolutely. Meeting him was inspiring. He was a man who dedicated himself to his organization. So, who knows, I might follow in his footsteps and get involved in the grass roots side of things. There's a million possibilities."

"So, you can't see yourself ever not being involved?"

"No. Not at this point. You know, I joke about retiring with a fishing rod and a beer and that day will come, but I'm not ready for that yet. I still have a burning desire to help the country and to serve the people. And I can't imagine that fire going away any time soon."

"That's a good thing," Nutley said. "The country certainly needs you."

For the next hour, Nutley questioned, reminisced, and laughed with his guest. As the hour came to a close, he took a deep breath and basked in the ecstasy of his finest show.

He was back on top.

"Senator," Nutley said, "on behalf of the country, I want to thank you."

"You played a pretty big role in this too," Brightman said. "So, before I leave, I have something for you. A little memento." He pulled a hemp string with a cut silver dollar medallion from his pocket and hung it around Nutley's neck.

Nutley swallowed hard and extended his hand to shake. "Thank you."

Brightman grabbed it in his own with a firm grip.

As their hands locked, Nutley's stomach fluttered. He looked down. At his leg. It tingled.

***

Dr. Gress stepped from the woods into the clearing. Living off the land, without access to civilization, left him unsure of what day it was and unaware of what had transpired with the giants.

The remains of Joros's mansion, now a smoldering ruin, lay ahead.

Gress remembered the majestic view it had once been, and his stomach knotted knowing he had caused the downfall of something so pristine. It wasn't supposed to happen this way. He was creating perfection, not destroying it.

As he approached the rubble, he recognized some of the broken fragments protruding from the pile. He scaled halfway up the mountain of debris and uncovered shattered remnants of the chandelier that once hung above the house's atrium. He dug around further and found an arm of the leatherback chair he had sat in earlier. As he moved some scraps, he caught a passing glimpse of his reflection in a shattered piece of mirror. Unnerved by what he thought he saw, he pulled the shard up to get a better look at himself--but immediately dropped the glass in horror. Gone was his thick wavy hair, his high cheek bones, and lean muscular physique. His potions had worn off.

The sound of paper snapping in the wind grabbed his ear. Relieved to have something else to focus on, he followed the sound, working his way up a mound of cracked marble and stepping over the albino gorilla rug, which was now black with soot, until he was at the highest point on the mountain of rubble. A section of his notes, trapped between chunks of ruin, flapped in the breeze.

He pulled the papers out, cleared a place to sit, and leafed through the pages of his work. Something on the handwritten page jumped out at him. He rubbed dust off the paper and squinted, examining the equation that formed the basis of his life's work.

He looked up, calculating in his head, furiously drawing numbers in the air with his finger, summing, dividing, and carrying. When he was through, he shook his head in disbelief and recalculated. Then re-recalculated. The re-re-recalculated.

His calculations were off. His potions weren't stable, and never could be. It was an impossibility. He sat, stunned, staring into the distance until a rustle from the bottom of the rubble mountain caught his attention.

Scourge Joros climbed the ruins of his mansion. He lost a shoe on the way up and, by the time he reached the top, his suit was covered in grime and filth. When he reached the top, he sat next to the doctor.

"There was a mistake in the work," Gress said. He looked at Joros who, still dumbfounded at the sight beneath him, was not listening.

"It's right here, see?" Gress pointed to the flawed equation, eager to explain the problem.

An expressionless Joros finally turned, landing his empty eyes on the papers in Gress's hand. He sneered and slapped the work from the doctor's grip.

Gress reached out to catch what he could, grabbing one page as the rest scattered and floated down the hill. He stared at the sheet in his hand--an old hypothesis he had not paid any mind in almost two decades. It was interesting. But could the premise be valid?

He stood straight and began computing, working out the problem by writing with his finger in the air.

"What are you doing?" Joros said in annoyance. "Stop that."

"Of course," Gress said to himself. "We can't implant foreign DNA." He shut his eyes and continued speaking to himself, but out loud. "The subject's DNA must be manipulated."

"Manipulated?" Joros said, suddenly interested.

"Traits cannot be transferred between individuals. Each person's genetic slate must be wiped clean. Each gene must be reduced to a common, albeit very basic, expression of that gene."

Joros looked at Gress with confusion.

"We can't make everyone perfect," Gress said. "But I believe we can minimize everyone's genetic variation."

"So we can make everyone ... the same?"

"There would still be very slight differences, of course. Although, even they would fade after a few generations." Gress let the idea sink in. If everyone were the same, then no one was inferior. If no one was inferior, then wasn't everyone perfect? He smiled. "Do you have any idea what this means?"

Joros smiled too. "Yes. I do."

***

Nutley marched up the steps of the brick elementary school which, surprisingly, had only taken minor damage from the giants. Once inside the school's auditorium, he scanned the tables and approached the one with an "M–Q" card hanging from the front. "Nutley," he said to the woman at the table.

She fingered through the ledger and spun the book to him.

He signed his name and then marched across the room into the voting booth. As he closed the curtain behind him, the excitement that had been building in him all morning culminated in a giant, impossible-to-contain smile.

He pulled a pen from his shirt pocket, clicked it to set out the tip, and cast his vote for president of the United States on the write-in line: Bart Brightman.

By the time polls had closed that evening, a landslide majority had done the same.

*** THE END ***

Thank you for reading. I hope you enjoyed the story. If so, please share your thoughts.

You can find me at:
Twitter: @rkdelka
Facebook: www.facebook.com/rkdelka
Website: www.rkdelka.com

And be sure to check out:

Thanks again,
R. K. Delka